FAIRY STORIES

retold by Jane Carruth

introduction by Julie Andrews

Cathay Books

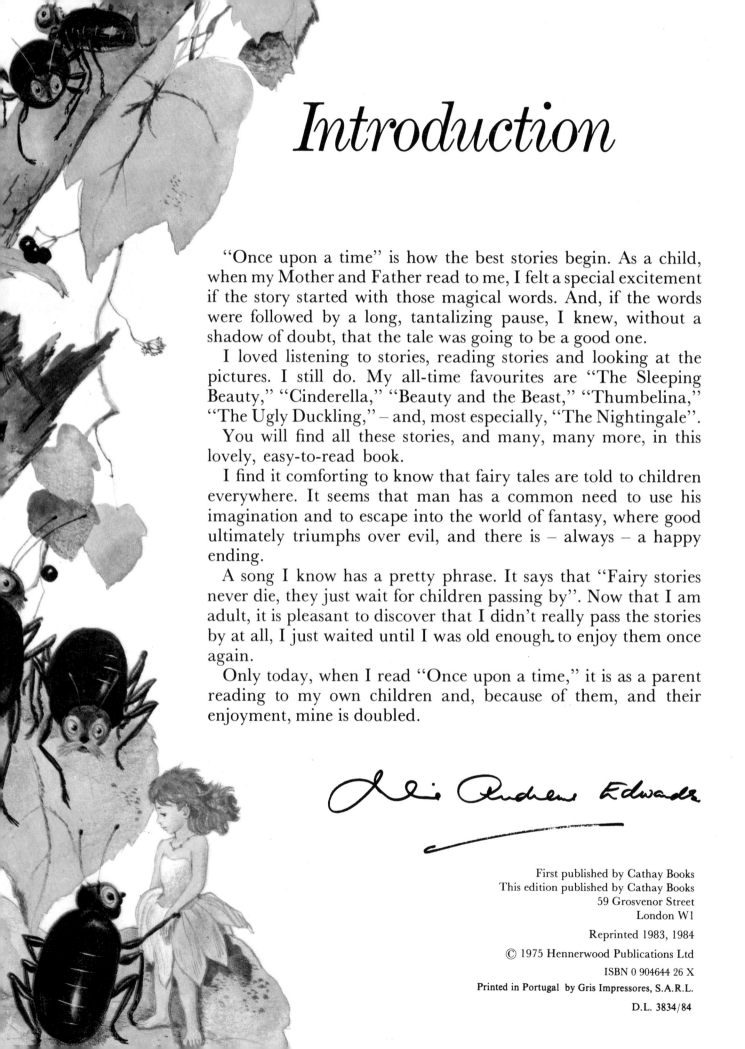

Introduction

"Once upon a time" is how the best stories begin. As a child, when my Mother and Father read to me, I felt a special excitement if the story started with those magical words. And, if the words were followed by a long, tantalizing pause, I knew, without a shadow of doubt, that the tale was going to be a good one.

I loved listening to stories, reading stories and looking at the pictures. I still do. My all-time favourites are "The Sleeping Beauty," "Cinderella," "Beauty and the Beast," "Thumbelina," "The Ugly Duckling," – and, most especially, "The Nightingale".

You will find all these stories, and many, many more, in this lovely, easy-to-read book.

I find it comforting to know that fairy tales are told to children everywhere. It seems that man has a common need to use his imagination and to escape into the world of fantasy, where good ultimately triumphs over evil, and there is – always – a happy ending.

A song I know has a pretty phrase. It says that "Fairy stories never die, they just wait for children passing by". Now that I am adult, it is pleasant to discover that I didn't really pass the stories by at all, I just waited until I was old enough to enjoy them once again.

Only today, when I read "Once upon a time," it is as a parent reading to my own children and, because of them, and their enjoyment, mine is doubled.

Julie Andrews Edwards

First published by Cathay Books
This edition published by Cathay Books
59 Grosvenor Street
London W1

Reprinted 1983, 1984

© 1975 Hennerwood Publications Ltd

ISBN 0 904644 26 X

Printed in Portugal by Gris Impressores, S.A.R.L.

D.L. 3834/84

Contents

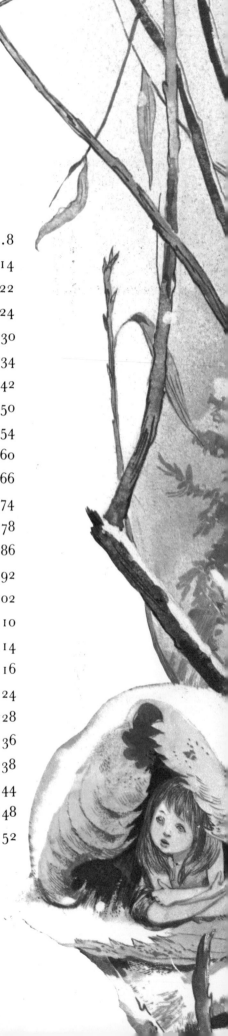

Puss-in-Boots

ONCE UPON A TIME there was a miller who had three sons. When he died his sons were disappointed to find that he had left them very little.

"I'll take the mill," said the eldest son. "It's mine by rights."

"I'll take the donkey," said the second son.

"And that leaves me with the cat," said the youngest son. "There is nothing else."

The miller's youngest son felt very sorry for himself. His brothers had not come off too badly for they would work the mill together. But now here he was with no money and only a cat for company. "Of course I could always sell you," he said, looking at the cat. "But then you would scarcely fetch the price of a good supper."

"I wouldn't do that if I were you," said

the cat. "I can be of great service to you."

Now, strange to say, the miller's son felt no surprise that he owned a talking cat. All he said was, "I don't see how a cat can help me to mend my fortunes."

"All I need," went on the cat, ignoring the interruption, "is a pair of fine high boots and a sack. That's not much to ask."

Now the cat spoke so earnestly that the young man began to believe in him. So he said, "Oh, very well, I'll find money somewhere to buy you the boots and as for the sack – that's easy!"

Puss was delighted with his fine red boots and when the miller's son gave him a hat as well, he vowed he had the kindest master in the world. Then away he went with the sack slung across his back. His master watched him go and he couldn't help wondering if he would ever set eyes on him again.

What do you think Puss-in-Boots meant to do with the sack? Well, first he filled it with lettuce and sweet-smelling bran – just the kind of food little rabbits like. Then he took it into the fields and lay down beside it, pretending to be fast asleep. But Puss-in-Boots wasn't really asleep. He was wide awake and holding a string fixed round the opening to the sack.

No sooner did a plump young rabbit come along than it smelt the bran and hopped into the sack. Puss pulled the string and the rabbit was caught!

Now the King was very fond of rabbit pie and Puss made straight for the palace. When he stood before the King he bowed low, and offered him the rabbit as a gift.

"What a very kind thought!" said the King. "Do tell me the name of your master."

"Oh yes, of course," said Puss-in-Boots, thinking quickly. "He is the Marquis of Carabas, Your Majesty. "The Marquis of Carabas, a very noble lord!"

"Indeed!" replied the King, pulling at his beard. "I must meet him."

Well, that was the first of many visits cunning Puss paid to the King's palace and, one day, he heard that the King meant to take his beautiful daughter for a drive along by the river, in his carriage.

Puss hurriedly left the palace and ran back to his master. "Quick!" he ordered. "Go down to the river and take a bathe."

By this time, Puss's master was quite used to obeying his clever cat so off he went to the river, took off his ragged clothes and plunged into the water. Puss hid the rags under a stone and then waited for the

King's carriage to pass. When he saw it coming, he began shouting, "Help, help! My master is drowning! Save him! Save the noble Marquis of Carabas!"

The King was only too happy to oblige, and after his coachman had dragged the miller's son out of the river, Puss whispered in the King's ear that thieves had stolen all his master's fine clothes. So then the King sent back to the palace for one of his own suits which fitted the young man rather badly but nevertheless made him look very handsome. At least the beautiful Princess thought so as the miller's son shyly seated himself by her side in the royal carriage. But then, of course, she

didn't really know who he was!

Meanwhile Puss-in-Boots was running along the road for all he was worth. But when he came to a fine golden meadow where some labourers were working, he stopped. "The King will soon be passing this way," he said fiercely. "If you don't tell him these meadows belong to the Marquis of Carabas, I'll come back and chop you up into mincemeat."

Puss looked as if he meant every word and the labourers agreed at once to do what he asked. Twice more Puss stopped and always he looked so fierce and threatening that the men working in the fields promised at once to say that all the land belonged to the Marquis of Carabas, should the King ask.

And of course the King *did* ask, stopping his carriage no less than three times to enquire. As each time he got the same answer, he began to look at the young man at his daughter's side with more and more admiration and respect. "How rich he must be!" he thought. "Hmm! Well!"

Puss-in-Boots was now far ahead of the King and his companions and presently he came to a magnificent castle which he happened to know belonged to a very bad-tempered ogre. This knowledge did not, however, prevent him from entering the castle to seek out the ogre.

"I simply had to come and see you," Puss began. "I just had to find out if you really did have the power to change yourself into any animal you wished."

The ogre sprawled in his huge gold chair and smiled down on the cat. There was nothing he enjoyed more than showing off, and Puss's tone was very respectful.

12

"Certainly I do," said the ogre proudly. "I can change myself into a lion or an elephant at the drop of a hat."

"Remarkable!" exclaimed Puss. "It's an honour to be talking to you. I wonder now if you would find it just as easy to become something really small, like – like a mouse?"

"Nothing easier," chuckled the ogre. "Do you doubt that I can?"

"No," Puss admitted, but he managed to sound very doubtful indeed, and that show-off ogre had to prove himself.

This was just what Puss-in-Boots had been waiting for and, as soon as the tiny mouse scampered over the floor, Puss pounced on it and gobbled it up.

So that was the end of the boastful ogre. Now Puss had the grand castle all to himself. After making certain that the table in the huge dining hall was suitably laid for three, he ran to the gates to wait for the King.

As soon as the royal coach appeared, Puss waved it to a standstill. "Welcome to my lord's castle," said he to the King. "Pray step this way." And he led the King and the Princess into the dining hall. His master tried in vain to get a word with his clever cat, but Puss winked broadly and prodded him into the chair next to the lovely Princess.

Well, by the end of the meal, the Princess was more than half in love with the miller's son and he with her. And when the Princess whispered to her father that there was no man she liked better, the King willingly gave his consent to the marriage.

So the miller's youngest son married the King's daughter and very happy he was too. As for Puss-in-Boots – he never had to catch another mouse! He had salmon and cream every day, and he slept on a velvet cushion.

Snow-White and Rose-Red

NCE UPON A TIME there were two pretty and loving sisters called Snow-White and Rose-Red. They were named after their mother's two favourite rose trees which bore white and red roses the whole year round.

Their mother was a widow and very poor, and their cottage was small and lonely for it stood on the edge of a deep forest. But the sisters knew the forest well and were never afraid to go there.

Snow-White and Rose-Red loved the long winter evenings almost as much as the hot summer days they spent in the forest. It was fun to sit round the fire and listen to the stories of adventure and romance which their mother read to them from a big red book.

One cold, wintry night, when the windows were thick with frost and snow covered the ground like a soft white carpet, the girls begged their mother to bring out the red book of romantic tales and read to them.

Their mother settled herself in her chair, and put on her spectacles. Then Snow-White gave her the big book, and she began to read.

Suddenly, above the noise of the wind, there came a loud knocking on the door, which made them all start.

"Who can it be?" Snow-White asked in a frightened voice. "Surely no one would visit us in such a storm?"

"Most likely some poor traveller has lost his way in the forest," her mother said, closing the book and taking off her spectacles. "Go to the door, child, and make him welcome."

"I'll go," said Rose-Red, who was bolder and braver than her sister. But, it was no ordinary traveller at the door, for there, on the step stood a huge brown bear!

"Mother – it's – it's a bear!" Rose-Red stammered. "A great brown bear. . . ."

Before her mother could reply, the bear spoke, "Don't be afraid," he said. "I mean you no harm. All I ask is that you invite me in to share your fire."

There was something so sad and gentle about his voice that Rose-Red found herself holding open the door and saying, "Poor thing! You're covered with snow. Very well, come inside and I'll brush the snow from your coat."

Snow-White tried to hide behind her mother's chair at the sight of the huge bear, but her mother told her that it was plain the bear meant them no harm.

"Warm some milk for the poor creature," said the old lady, "and make room for him by the hearth."

The bear growled contentedly as Snow-White offered him a saucerful of milk and when she saw how truly gentle he was, she could not stop herself from stroking his brown head. "Poor bear! It must have been awful for you out there in all that snow," she murmured.

There was no more reading from the book of Golden Legends that night for, as the hours passed, Snow-White and Rose-Red lost all fear of the huge bear. He was so gentle and friendly that they soon began to play with him, tugging at his shaggy coat and hiding thimbles and cotton reels under his huge paws.

"You are welcome to sleep here on the hearth," said their mother, when it was time to go to bed.

"And I'll come down early in the morning and unbolt the door to let you out," Snow-White promised.

After that first evening, the bear came many times to the cottage and the girls grew to look forward to his visits and even to love him. Now the door was never bolted, and the bear came in and out just as a friend would. But always, early in the morning, he left the cottage and trotted across the snow into the forest.

At the end of the winter, the bear told them that his visits to the cottage had come to an end. "I must now keep guard over my treasure," he said. "In the winter, when the ground is frozen hard, the forest dwarfs must stay underground. But in the spring, they take to wandering through the forest in search of anything they can steal. They are wicked and cunning and already they have stolen much of what rightfully belongs to me."

Snow-White and Rose-Red were sad to see their friend go. "We shall never forget you," Snow-White declared. "And there will always be a place for you on the hearth."

As soon as the bear had disappeared into the forest, the sisters helped their mother

to tidy the cottage. Then they went out to gather firewood.

It was not long before Rose-Red spied a tree that had been blown down by the wind and with a glad cry, she ran towards it.

"Don't go too close," Snow-White warned her sister, taking hold of her arm and pulling her back. "There's something odd beside that tree. Something that's hopping up and down – why, I know what it is! It's a tiny little man!"

"So it is!" Rose-Red exclaimed. "And look! His long white beard is holding him fast to the tree trunk. He's trying to pull himself free!"

As the girls drew closer, the little man caught sight of them. "Don't just stand there!" he screamed. "Idiots! Fools! Can't you see what has happened? I'm

caught by my beard?"

Rose-Red bent down and began tugging at the beard but no matter how hard she pulled she could not set it free.

"It's really caught fast in the crevice," she said at last. "I don't know how we can help."

"There's only one way," said Snow-White. And she got out her scissors and, snip, snap, she cut off at least two inches of beard.

The dwarf leapt high in the air, then began to storm, "You've ruined my beautiful white beard. You've cut off the end. What idiots you are! May you have bad luck for the rest of your days." And with that, he turned away and picking up a sack filled with gold, slung it over his shoulders, and made off into the bushes.

"Well!" exclaimed Rose-Red. "He wasn't very grateful, was he?"

"He was horrid," said Snow-White. "I'm sure I shall have a nightmare about him. Did you see how his little red eyes glittered with spite?"

But the sisters soon forgot the dwarf as they set about collecting firewood for their mother and, by the end of the morning, they were laughing and singing as they ran back to the cottage.

The very next day, however, they were to come upon the little man again. The sun was shining in a blue sky as they made their way to the stream where sometimes they liked to fish. Suddenly, Snow-White grasped her sister's arm. "Look!" she whispered, "It's that nasty dwarf again. But what on earth can he be doing? It's just as if something was pulling him into the water."

"I know!" Rose-Red cried. "That long white beard of his has tangled with his fishing line. Instead of catching a fish, the fish has caught him!"

When the dwarf saw the girls, he yelled, "Do something before that monster fish drags me into the water. Can't you see what's happening? Why are humans so stupid?"

"Of course we'll try and help," said Rose-Red. And she put her arms round the little man's waist and began to pull. But the fish thought it was battling for its life and was ready to put up a great fight.

"It's no use," Rose-Red said, at last. "I can't really hold you properly because you are so small."

"Idiot!" snapped the dwarf. "Think of something . . ." he broke off, as he felt himself slipping closer and closer to the water's edge.

"There's only one thing to do," said Snow-White. And she took out her scissors and, snip, snap, cut another few inches off the little man's white beard.

The fish fell back into the water with a huge splash, and the little man rolled over and over in the mud. When at last he scrambled to his feet, he was speechless with anger. Then he moaned, "My beautiful, beautiful beard! Bad luck to you both! May you turn into toadstools!"

And with that, he groped among the reeds until he found his sack and dragged it away behind a tree.

When the dwarf was out of sight, Rose-Red whispered, "That sack was filled with pearls! I wish we knew where he was taking it."

"I'm almost sorry we came to his rescue," said Snow-White. "That's twice we have saved him and all we got for our pains was his threat to turn us into toadstools. You don't suppose . . ."

"No, of course not!" Rose-Red laughed.

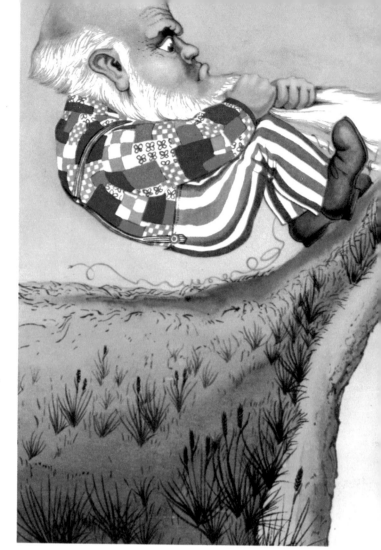

"That horrid little man hasn't any power over us. Just the same, we won't tell mother about him. It would only worry her."

"Perhaps we had better stay at home for a few days," her sister remarked, as Rose-Red cast her line into the stream. "The forest seems quite different these days."

Two weeks passed before once again Snow-White and Rose-Red ventured into the forest.

"I want you to go to the village and buy me some silks and cottons," their mother said to them, one sunny morning. "I need the cotton for mending so please don't be too long. Take the short cut through the forest and try to be back before dinner."

To their relief, the sisters saw no sign of

"Goodness! He'll be carried away!" Snow-White cried. "Quick! Run! He's struggling so hard that the bird can't fly properly."

Rose-Red was the first to reach the dwarf and not a moment too soon for already he was being lifted off the ground. Catching hold of his legs, she hung on with all her strength. Then Snow-White arrived and together they tugged and pulled until, at last, the big bird, tiring of its game of tug-of-war, dropped the little man at their feet and flew away.

"That's the third time we have come to your rescue," Rose-Red said. "Perhaps this time you will show that you are grateful."

But the little man's face was scarlet with rage as he looked down at his torn jacket.

"Couldn't you do better than that!" he screamed. "My jacket is ruined and I've lost my hat. Imbeciles! Dolts! Idiots! You'll get no thanks from me!"

Then hopping over the grass, he began searching for his hat. The sisters watched him for a time, without offering to help. Then Snow-White saw the hat in a thorn bush and went over to get it. But the dwarf was there before her. "Leave it! Leave it!" he screamed.

"Let's go home," Rose-Red whispered. "Don't you see! The hat was close to another of his sacks. I'm sure I saw the glitter of diamonds as he tried to push it out of sight."

"I hope we have seen the last of him," said Snow-White. "All our happy days in the forest are spoilt now that he has come to live there."

But soon Rose-Red and Snow-White forgot all about the dwarf. Their mother became ill and there was more work than ever for them to do in the cottage.

the dwarf as they ran through the forest and, once in the village, they made their purchases and then set off for home.

Some way from their cottage, Snow-White was the first to notice a huge bird hovering in the sky, almost overhead.

"Look, Rose-Red," she whispered. "What an enormous bird! It's the biggest I've ever seen. And see how it hovers – just as if it were ready to swoop down and pounce on some poor, defenceless rabbit."

Rose-Red shivered. "Let's wait and watch what it does," she suggested.

As she spoke, the bird dropped like a stone out of the sky and when it rose again they saw, to their horror, that it held their old acquaintance, the dwarf, in its strong talons.

Every morning Snow-White went into the tiny garden and gathered roses, white and red, from the two rose trees, so that whenever her mother woke from a drowsy sleep, she would see the roses and smell their sweet perfume.

One evening, just as the sun was setting, the sisters left the cottage and went into the forest in search of firewood, so that they could make a fire. At long last, their mother was strong enough to leave her bed and come downstairs, but she must be kept warm.

As they looked around for suitable sticks, they came upon the dwarf again. But this time he was in no danger. He was staring down at the most wonderful,

shining jewels imaginable. Beside him lay some empty sacks and the diamonds, rubies and glistening pearls were all about his feet. Snow-White and Rose-Red stared in amazement. They stood perfectly still, scarcely daring to breathe at the sight of so much treasure.

Suddenly the ugly little man looked up and saw them. His wicked face grew dark red with rage and he began screaming at them in his shrill voice, "Spies! Thieves! You're after my treasure. Be off with you! May snakes grow out of your hair!"

So terrible was his anger that the girls clung to each other, unable to move. He was still screaming and shaking his tiny fist at them when suddenly there was a deep growl from behind some bushes.

With a gasp of fright, the dwarf tried frantically to stuff the jewels into one of the sacks and make off with it. But he was too late. From out of the bushes came a huge brown bear. And before the dwarf could dive into a nearby hole in the ground, the bear had scattered the precious stones and was standing over him.

"Noble Mr. Bear," the dwarf began to whine, cringing before him, "let me go about my business. Take these two wicked girls there. They are the ones who are after your treasure. Think what a tasty bite they will be for your dinner! Set me free and you will never see me again."

The bear paid no attention to the dwarf's frantic pleas. With a single blow from one of his huge paws, he knocked the wicked little man to the ground and there he lay, very still.

Snow-White and Rose-Red were so frightened that they tried to hide behind one of the trees. But the bear called to them, "Snow-White! Rose-Red! Have you forgotten me so soon? What of the happy evenings we spent together in the winter?"

"It's our very own bear!" Rose-Red whispered joyfully, "I am sure it must be. Come on, Snow-White, let's go to him. There is nothing to be afraid of now. The wicked dwarf is dead and the bear is our friend."

Hand in hand, the sisters ran to the bear. They saw him towering over the dwarf. And then, all at once, they found themselves looking at a tall handsome young man, magnificently dressed in brocade and velvet. Around his feet lay the bear-skin.

"Oh, oh!" gasped Rose-Red. "You're not a bear, not a real bear after all!" And she sounded so disappointed that the young man laughed.

"No," he said. "I am a King's son. This wicked dwarf, who now lies dead, bewitched me and stole most of my treasure. The spell could not be broken except by his death."

"Then we have lost our friend of the long winter months," Snow-White said shyly. "A King's son would never want to visit us in our humble cottage."

"A King's son might have lost his heart already to the dearest, loveliest girl in the world," he told her, smiling.

"That's you!" Rose-Red cried, for she guessed that the Prince had fallen in love with her gentle sister.

And so it proved. The Prince came back to the cottage and when the widow heard the whole story, she gave Snow-White her blessing.

Snow-White married her Prince amid great splendour and – what do you think – the Prince's handsome brother fell head over heels in love with Rose-Red.

Soon it was Rose-Red's turn to be a royal bride, and to live in the palace with her sister.

One day the sisters, in their grand dresses, came to the cottage for their mother.

"You are to stay with us in the palace," they told her. "It's all arranged and, what's more, you shall have a room whose windows look out on to a beautiful garden of your very own."

Can you guess what pleased the widow most as she sat by the window of her splendid room? I'll tell you. Two slender rose trees – one white and the other red – the very same which had bloomed for so many years in front of her humble cottage.

The Shoemaker and the Elves

HERE WAS ONCE a good and honest shoemaker who prided himself on making very fine shoes. The shoemaker worked hard but the day came when he found he had no money to pay for the soft leather he always used.

"I have only one piece of leather left," he told his wife sadly.

His wife tried to comfort her husband. Then she said, "Why not use what leather there is? Cut out the shoes and leave them on your work-bench until morning."

So the shoemaker shaped the soft leather and then went upstairs to bed.

Imagine his surprised delight in the morning when he found a pair of the finest shoes he had ever seen in his life waiting for him on the bench. He rubbed his eyes as he noted the tiny stitches. "Come, wife," he called in an excited voice. "Come and see my beautiful shoes!"

The shoes sold at once, and for a great deal of money, and the shoemaker ran to market and bought more leather. That night he cut out two more pairs and left them on his workbench. In the morning, there sat two pairs of shoes, superbly made. Later that morning, the shoemaker hugged himself with joy as he counted the gold he had got for them.

For weeks and weeks the invisible craftsmen continued to make the shoes while the shoemaker slept. Just before Christmas, his wife remarked, "How I long to know who makes our beautiful shoes. Let's hide in the workshop tonight and find out!"

Just as the clock chimed twelve – through the open window hopped two naked little men. They set to work on the leather immediately, hammering and stitching until all the shoes were made. Then they put down their tools and went soberly away.

"So now we know!" exclaimed the shoemaker's wife. "Poor little things! They were shivering with cold."

"We'll make clothes for them," declared

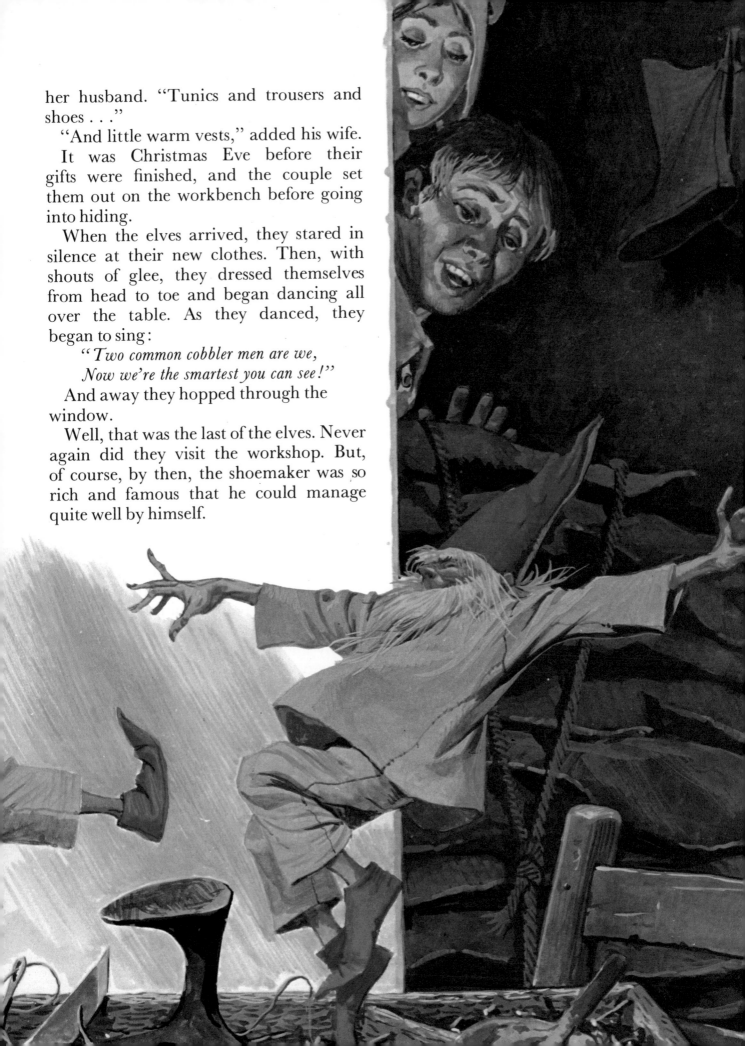

her husband. "Tunics and trousers and shoes . . ."

"And little warm vests," added his wife.

It was Christmas Eve before their gifts were finished, and the couple set them out on the workbench before going into hiding.

When the elves arrived, they stared in silence at their new clothes. Then, with shouts of glee, they dressed themselves from head to toe and began dancing all over the table. As they danced, they began to sing:

"Two common cobbler men are we,
Now we're the smartest you can see!"

And away they hopped through the window.

Well, that was the last of the elves. Never again did they visit the workshop. But, of course, by then, the shoemaker was so rich and famous that he could manage quite well by himself.

The Emperor's New Clothes

HERE WAS ONCE an Emperor – and you may be just like him – who loved wearing new clothes. So great was his passion for robes and ruffs and satin breeches that he spent all his money on them. And when that was finished, he was obliged to think up new taxes so that he could pay for his extravagant tastes.

His subjects knew perfectly well that the money they were obliged to give to the State was mostly used to keep their Emperor in new outfits. But the Emperor was a kindly man – not the 'off-with-his head' kind of Emperor – so they paid their taxes willingly and were quite proud when people came from far and wide to gaze at their gorgeously, over-dressed ruler.

Now this Emperor, unlike most, took very little interest in his army or his navy and they got on very well without him. Nor was he in the habit of visiting the theatre except, of course, to show off a particularly brilliant waistcoat or unusual hat.

One day, two rogues came to the town where the Emperor had his palace. It wasn't long before they heard all about the Emperor's passionate interest in clothes. And one said to the other, "We could do very well for ourselves if we set up as weavers and the Emperor heard about us." And he winked.

So the two rogues let it be known around the market place that they were weavers and that they had come specially to the town to weave a most wonderful cloth.

The Emperor soon heard about the two false weavers and they were summoned into his presence.

"Is it true that you have the power to weave a cloth the like of which has never before been seen?" demanded the Emperor, his eyes shining.

"Indeed yes," said the tallest of the two rogues. "Give us the chance and you shall have a suit more splendid than any you now possess."

"Set us up in the palace," said the other, who was small and fat. "Give us all the thread we require and you will be dazzled by the beauty of our cloth."

"It shall be done," cried the Emperor, clapping his podgy hands. "Move in today. Bring your baggage for you shall be my guests until the cloth is made."

The two rogues were highly delighted at this. They moved into the palace that same day, set up their looms and then went to the Emperor to tell him how much gold and blue and green silks they would require.

"There is just one thing, Your Imperial Majesty," said the tall black-haired rogue, and he bowed deeply. "No person who is stupid or unfit to hold high office will be able to see the wonderful material we are weaving."

"I understand," said the Emperor. And the rogues went off to await the gold

thread and costly silks.

For a whole week they sat at their empty looms pretending to weave and as, by now, everybody knew that you had to be clever and worthy of high office to see the beautiful cloth, those who visited them pretended to admire the cloth. They used words like, "colourful" and "gorgeous" and "splendid", before they backed out of the room.

Now, although the Emperor heard from his servants about the wonderful patterns and colours the weavers were producing, he had not yet sent any of his important ministers to view the cloth.

When the weavers fourth or was it fifth request for more gold thread arrived, the Emperor decided to send his most important Minister of Taxes to see how the weavers were progressing. "Report to me at once," he ordered the old man. "You are my most trusted official. If you are happy with their progress I shall be content."

The Minister of Taxes had held his office for many years. He felt greatly honoured at his Emperor's words and he determined to give a very honest report.

"I shall take my young assistant with me," he decided. "He's an expert on colours."

So the young man was told that he must accompany the Minister to the weavers' room and he blushed as red as his hair at the honour. He too resolved to note every colour and each intricate pattern.

As he walked sedately along the corridor – just two steps behind the Minister – the old man turned and said, "When we reach the weavers' room, I want you to go in and examine the cloth most particularly. You may feel it and test its quality."

"I understand," said the young man, and once again he blushed to the roots of his red hair.

The Minister of Taxes stood at the open door while the young man went up to the looms. Only one of the weavers was seated at the loom and he greeted the young man with a great show of enthusiasm. "The cloth is finished," he said. "Hold it up. Feel the quality. Are not the glowing colours truly wonderful?"

The old man watched carefully as the weaver pretended to give the cloth to his assistant. He saw the young man hold out his hands and then heard him exclaim, "Yes, yes, truly wonderful! Our Emperor will be highly delighted!"

"What's this?" thought the Minister of Taxes. "I can't see a thing! Can my old eyes be failing me at last?"

Then the young man called to him, "Come over here and see for yourself, Minister. The colours and the patterns are quite unique."

The weaver said nothing; he was rogue enough to know that pride makes even the most honest of men into fools. The young assistant to the Minister did not dare admit that he saw nothing in case the Minister declared he was a stupid idiot. And the old man did not dare speak the truth for fear his Emperor dismissed him from his high office.

"I will tell the Emperor that he may now be measured for the suit," said the Minister of Taxes. But his step was heavy as he made off down the corridor.

"Well?" demanded the Emperor, as soon as he saw his Minister again. "What about the cloth?"

"Er – ahem – very nice! Wonderful, in fact," said the old man. "The weavers are ready now to take your measurements, Your Majesty!"

Scarcely able to conceal his excitement, the Emperor sent for the two rogues. They came, armed with scissors and measures and one of them pretended to have in his arms a roll of the wonderful material.

"Admire it, Your Majesty!" he said. "If you do not, you will be alone among your courtiers."

"I do!" said the Emperor, blinking slightly for, of course, there was nothing to see. "Magnificent colours – you shall be well rewarded." And, as if to convince himself, he sent for a bag of gold and gave it to the false weavers.

What care they took with their measurements and when at last they had noted every single one, they promised the suit would be ready the very next day.

That night the Emperor slept uneasily believing that, above everything, he must take care to keep silent about what he saw, and what he did not see. "I cannot, will not be called a fool," he decided unhappily, as he tossed about.

In the morning he announced that he would parade through the streets in his wonderful new clothes so that all the people might gaze upon the splendour of their Emperor.

The weavers begged that they might be allowed to dress the Emperor themselves. And the foolish Emperor permitted them to pull on breeches he could not see or feel, and button up a waistcoat which they told him resembled the colouring of a bird of paradise.

When at last they announced the Emperor was ready, not one of the courtiers had the courage to speak the truth. One even went as far as to vow he had seen a pin in the Emperor's brilliant robe which must have been overlooked by the weavers.

With all the dignity he could muster, the Emperor took his place under the magnificent canopy.

Crowds lined the streets as slowly, oh so slowly, he began his processional walk. Above the blare of trumpets, the courtiers shouts could be heard, "Long live our noble Emperor! Long live the Emperor!"

Those who hoped for a high place at court shouted more loudly than the rest, and they added expressions like, "What splendid robes!" "Truly marvellous!"

But there was one among all the crowd who had the courage to speak his mind. This was a little boy who, pointing his finger at the Emperor, shrieked, "Look! Our Emperor is in his birthday suit! He has nothing on!"

The boy's high shrill laugh stirred the crowd to laughter. They took up his cry. And soon all the people lining the streets were laughing at their Emperor.

The Emperor walked on. There was nothing else he could do, but with each step, he was telling himself that never again would he pretend to see what was never there. He had learnt his lesson. And as the procession continued, the two rogues galloped out of the city, their saddle-bags stuffed with gold and costly silks, and their faces creased with mirth at the foolishness of proud men.

The Wolf and the Seven Kids

NCE UPON A TIME there was a wise old Mother Goat who had seven little kids. They lived in a cosy hut in the middle of a wood and were all very happy.

Mother Goat took great care of her children and scarcely ever left them alone for fear of a hungry wolf that roamed the forest. But one day, having run out of sugar, she made up her mind to go to the village to get some.

"Listen carefully," she said to her children, as she picked up her shopping basket. "As soon as I have gone, bolt the door. Let no one in until I return. If Wolf comes, you will know him by his deep, rough voice and his black feet."

Now it so happened that Wolf was hiding behind a tree watching the house. When he saw Mother Goat leave, he waited until she was out of sight, then ran over to the door.

"Open up, dear children," he called. "Your silly old mother has forgotten her purse."

But the kids knew it couldn't be their mother for the voice was too deep and too rough. So they called back, "Go away! Go away! We know from your deep rough voice that you are Wolf come to eat us, hair, skin and all!"

This made Wolf more than ever anxious to get at the little goats so he thought to himself, "I can make my voice soft with cough mixture." And off he went to the chemist's where he bought a large bottle of red sticky cough mixture. After swallowing a third of the bottle, he went back to the little house.

"Open up, dear children," he called in a voice which was quite soft and gentle. "Mother has brought you some lovely presents." And he was so eager to set eyes on the kids that he placed one of his big black paws on the bars of the tiny window.

"We won't open up," cried the little goats, as soon as they saw the big black foot. "Go away, Wolf! You can't fool us for we know you by your black feet!"

"So it's my black paws that have given

me away," thought Wolf, and he sat down to think. He thought and he thought until he thought of the old mill and the fat little miller who baked his own white bread.

Away went Wolf to the miller. "Put some dough on my paws and then sprinkle them with flour," ordered Wolf, showing all his big teeth.

The miller trembled. He was sure Wolf was up to no good but he was too frightened to say what was in his mind. So he brought out the dough, spread it over the wolf's feet and then dabbed on the white flour.

Away went Wolf and soon, for the third time, he was knocking at Mother Goat's door.

"Open up, dear children," he called softly. "Mother is here and her basket is full of lovely presents."

"Show us your feet," called back the kids, "so that we can see if they are white."

Wolf went to the window and put his white paws to the bars.

"It must be our own mother this time," the kids told each other, as soon as they saw the white feet. "Let's open the door and see what presents she has for us."

But, oh dear! As soon as the door was opened, in rushed hungry Wolf. One little kid dived into the wash-tub; another hid under the table. The third crept into the broom cupboard and the fourth, fifth and sixth jumped into bed. But Wolf found them all and gobbled them up there and then. Only the seventh and youngest little goat escaped, having shut himself inside the clock case.

In fear and trembling, the little goat waited until he heard Wolf leave the hut. Then he sat down by the open door to wait for his mother.

Poor old Mother Goat wept bitterly when she returned home and heard the whole sad story from her youngest son. She had no heart to tidy the hut which was all topsy-turvy after Wolf's visit. "We'll go out for a walk," she said, taking her youngest by the hand. "I can't stay here without thinking about your poor brothers."

It was the saddest kind of outing the little

kid had ever been on, for his mother cried all the way to the big tree where they usually had their picnics. Then, what do you think, the little kid saw Wolf himself! There he was under the tree, and snoring so loudly that the branches trembled.

"Look at his stomach!" the little kid whispered. "It's all big and round and full of MY brothers!"

"Indeed it is," said Mother Goat, peering at the wolf's huge, bulging stomach. "Upon my horns, I do believe it's moving. Quick fetch me my scissors, cotton and needle for your brothers are inside,

struggling to get out."

The little kid flew back to the house and fetched the scissors, cotton and needle. Then Mother Goat, who had been an excellent dressmaker in her younger days, slit open Wolf's stomach as he slept.

Out popped one little kid, quickly followed by another and another. In no time at all Mother Goat's family was once again complete. And still Wolf snored on.

Now fetch me some stones from the river," Mother Goat commanded. And the kids scampered away. Soon, Mother Goat had filled Wolf's stomach with stones, stitched it neatly together again, and was on her way home. But not until they were safely inside and the door bolted did Mother Goat permit her children to dance and sing and hug each other. Then she used some of her sugar to make them toffee apples for their tea.

But what happened to the wicked wolf? Well, he slept on until it was nearly dark. Then feeling unusually heavy and very thirsty, he made his way to the stream for a nice long drink. You can guess what happened! The stones in his stomach made him lose his balance as he bent down to drink and he fell into the water and was drowned.

Mother Goat is quite often seen in the village these days for now that Wolf is dead she knows she can safely leave her seven little kids to play by themselves.

Cinderella

ONCE UPON A TIME there was a rich man who had everything he wanted in the world. He had a loving wife, a very pretty young daughter and a fine house, which had cost a fortune.

The day came, however, when his wife fell seriously ill and, after only a short time, she died. The rich man became so sad that he no longer cared so much about his fine house or even his young daughter. He went on long trips abroad and, on one of these trips, he met a good-looking widow who had two rather ugly daughters.

Now, the widow thought it would be a feather in her cap to capture such a rich man and she set about persuading him that he should marry again.

"I have a daughter," the rich man told her, "who is very dear to me."

"I shall be her second mother," promised the widow, "and my own two daughters will be like sisters to her."

At last the rich man decided to marry the widow and take her home. His new wife was charmed with the fine house, but she took an instant dislike to her step-daughter. She was so much prettier than her own two daughters and her dresses were much grander.

Now, the rich man was quite taken in by his wife and he thought that once again he would be master of a happy little family.

"I shall be away on business for quite a time," he told his daughter, one day, "but your stepmother and your two new sisters will be company for you."

No sooner had he left the house than his wife and her daughters showed their true natures.

"Now that your father is no longer here to protect you," the stepmother sneered, "you will take off that grand dress!" And she pushed the rich man's daughter into the bedroom and threw at her a pile of clothing which only a servant-girl would wear.

"Yes, do as mother says," cried one of the Ugly Sisters. "From now on your place is in the kitchen and don't dare to forget it!"

"Let's give her a name which will help her to remember her duties," suggested the other Ugly Sister. "Let's called her Cinderella. After all, she's going to spend a great deal of her time cleaning out the fires and grubbing among the cinders."

Poor Cinderella – how unhappy her life became for her stepmother and stepsisters treated her as their slave.

One day, a messenger from the royal palace came to the door. He delivered a large white card on which were printed the words: *You are invited to the Grand Ball which His Royal Highness, the Prince, is giving at the Palace.*

The invitation threw the Ugly Sisters into such a state of excitement that they nearly fainted. Their mother soon revived them, however, with smelling salts and, as she fussed over them, she shouted for Cinderella.

"Yes, we must have Cinderella," said one of the sisters, as she sat up. "She must curl our hair, iron our ribbons and polish

our slippers."

The Ball was to be held the very next night and for the rest of the day poor Cinderella was kept so busy that she had no time even to sit among the cinders.

"Cinderella – do this!"

"Cinderella – do that!"

From early morning to late at night she was ordered about by the two Ugly Sisters.

The next evening the sisters, dressed in the finest gowns that money could buy, prepared to set out for the palace. Not a word of thanks did they give Cinderella as they swept away.

"Just make sure you wash that kitchen floor before we return," one of them shouted from the hallway.

Cinderella waited until the door banged, then she sat down in the kitchen and began to cry. "If only I had a chance to go to that Ball," she thought. "How I long to see the Prince for myself!"

35

As she sat there silently weeping, her bucket and broom forgotten, there was a sudden flash of light and there stood before her the most beautiful lady she had ever seen. "You want to go to the Ball, Cinderella," said she, "and so you shall! I am your fairy godmother with the power to make your dearest wish come true."

Then the fairy told Cinderella to go into the garden and fetch her a pumpkin. Scarcely daring to look at the gracious fairy, Cinderella hastened to obey. She chose the biggest, fattest pumpkin she could find. Her godmother took it into the carriageway, touched it with her silver wand and, lo and behold, there stood a magnificent coach of solid gold!

"Now fetch me the mousetrap," she told the astonished girl. And when Cinderella did so, she tapped the four plump mice inside with her wand and, lo and behold, they changed into prancing horses.

Cinderella rubbed her eyes in amazement. But more wonderful things were still to happen. Four green lizards, hiding behind the water-barrel, became four splendid footmen, and a frisky young rat was transformed into a smart coachman, who took his place on the wonderful coach.

"I-I shall be like a real Princess with a golden coach and footmen!" Cinderella whispered. Then, glancing down at her ragged dress, she added softly, "But how all these grand lords and ladies will laugh when they see my rags!"

"They will not laugh!" declared the fairy, and tapping her godchild on the shoulder, she changed her rags into the most gorgeous, fantastically beautiful dress you can imagine.

As Cinderella touched the gossamer-like skirt, her godmother handed her two dainty glass slippers. "Wear these," she commanded, "and you will charm the Prince with your graceful dancing."

Now, Cinderella was ready for the Ball. She seated herself in the splendid coach and the coachman gathered up the reins.

"Wait!" said her godmother and, for once, her voice was stern. "Remember this, Cinderella. You must leave the Ball before the clock strikes twelve. Disobey me, and your wonderful dress will turn to rags. There will be no fine coach awaiting you; only an old pumpkin and four little mice. Do you understand?"

"I understand," said Cinderella, "and I promise to obey you, dear godmother."

As soon as Cinderella drove up to the palace, the sight of her magnificent gold coach and her own beauty as she stepped out of it, made everyone think she must be a Princess.

A servant ran to prepare the Prince. "Your Highness," he gasped, "she must be a royal personage from a far country for we have never set eyes on her until now."

Greatly interested, the Prince went to meet this strange Princess. He could hardly take his eyes off her as he led her into the great ballroom and begged her to dance with him.

What a handsome couple they made as they circled round! Cinderella, her eyes shining like stars, was as light as thistle-down in the Prince's arms.

"Who is she?" the Ugly Sisters asked each other enviously. "She must be one of these foreign Princesses. None of our dressmakers could make a dress like the one she's wearing."

"He can't take his eyes off her," said

one of their friends, jealously.

And the Ugly Sisters pulled faces behind their fans and felt quite sorry for themselves. "It's plain he's not going to have time for us," said one.

"I'm going to get an even grander dress for the Ball tomorrow night," said the other.

As the evening wore on, the Prince danced only with Cinderella. Although he questioned her about herself, her only answer was a smile so radiant that the poor young man forgot his question. And begged her to continue smiling at him! And this, Cinderella was more than willing to do for she, too, was already half in love.

Just when she was wishing the night would last forever, the palace clock struck a quarter to twelve. Suddenly, Cinderella remembered her promise to the fairy, and hurriedly making a curtsey to her royal partner, she ran from the glittering ballroom.

Too excited to think of bed, Cinderella whose wonderful dress had changed to her patched old frock as she entered the silent house, waited up for the Ugly Sisters.

"We would have brought you out of bed in any case," they told her, as soon as they came home, "for we need you to attend to us."

"Did you have a nice time?" Cinderella asked, hiding a smile.

"No, we did not," snapped one of the sisters. "The Prince had no eyes for us at all. There was some upstart of a girl who kept the Prince all to herself. Even when she left, he still refused to dance with any of us."

"Anyway, we'll have another chance tomorrow," said the second sister. "He's giving a second Ball, and as long as that

Princess doesn't turn up, we shall no doubt enjoy ourselves."

Cinderella put away their gowns and ribbons and gave them hot drinks and when at last they told her she could go to bed, she thanked them, adding, "I suppose I couldn't go to the Ball tomorrow night? I would be happy to wear one of your old dresses!"

"What!" the sisters exclaimed in one voice, and then they looked at each other and burst out laughing.

"You'll be asking us next if you can ride in our carriage when we go shopping," said the elder of the sisters, as they shut the door on Cinderella. "Oh, go to bed!"

The next day, Cinderella was busier than ever helping the Ugly Sisters to prepare for the second night of the Ball. And by the time they had left she was so tired that she sank on to a stool in the kitchen. She closed her eyes and began to dream that she was in the Prince's arms.

"Do you want very much to go to the Ball a second time?"

The voice roused her from her dreams. There was her fairy godmother standing before her.

"Oh, godmother!" Cinderella cried, "If only I could!"

"You will go to the Ball and in a dress even more lovely than before," promised the fairy, as she touched the girl with her wand.

"Remember my warning," she said, as she helped Cinderella into the golden coach. "You must leave before twelve strikes."

The Prince was waiting eagerly for his mysterious Princess to arrive and no sooner did he see her than he took her in his arms.

"I have thought only of this moment,"

he whispered, as he led her on to the floor. As the golden hours flew past, Cinderella forgot all about the time. It was only when the first stroke of midnight sounded that she remembered her godmother's warning.

With no word of explanation, she broke away from the astonished Prince and rushed out of the ballroom. Down the long marble steps she fled, like a frightened white bird and as she ran she lost one of her dainty glass slippers.

Alas, long before she reached the palace gates, her wonderful dress had changed to rags. There was no golden carriage waiting to take her home but in the gutter a fat yellow pumpkin lay forlornly on its side.

Blinded with tears, Cinderella stumbled

along the dark streets, never noticing that four little mice were following her all the way home.

The next morning, the Ugly Sisters could talk of little else but the vanishing Princess. "You should have seen how she ran!" they sniggered, "and that fool of a Prince ran after her."

"Did-did he find her?" Cinderella asked timidly.

"He did not!" one of the Ugly Sisters exclaimed. "All he found was her glass slipper, which he sat gazing at for the rest of the evening!"

Later that same day, heralds from the palace came riding into town with a proclamation from the Prince. It set the Ugly Sisters chattering like monkeys for it announced that the Prince would marry the girl who could wear a certain glass slipper!

"Goodness – it might well be me!" cried one sister. "My feet are really very slender, you know!"

"They're broader and dumpier than mine!" shouted her sister.

As they argued, a steward, bearing the glass slipper on a velvet cushion, arrived at their house.

"I'm first!" declared the elder sister. And she began pushing and pulling in her frantic efforts to squeeze her foot into the tiny slipper. It was all in vain, and her younger sister, faring no better, ordered the steward out of the house. But he had noticed Cinderella and he insisted that she, too, try the slipper.

No need to tell you it was a perfect fit and as the steward prepared to take Cinderella to the palace, who should appear but the fairy godmother!

"You shall go to your Prince dressed as a Princess," she pronounced, touching the

girl with her silver wand.

When he saw Cinderella in her lovely dress, the Prince was more than ever enchanted with her, and he arranged to marry her the very next day.

Far too happy to be angry with the spiteful sisters, Cinderella invited them to the wedding. But when they saw her standing beside the handsome, adoring Prince, they choked with rage and jealousy and had to leave before the end of the ceremony.

Never again did Cinderella have need of her wonderful godmother for the Prince loved her so much that he devoted all his days to making her happy.

Hansel and Gretel

O NCE UPON A TIME, after a hard, cruel winter and a summer in which no rain fell, there was not enough food for everybody. Only the rich could afford to buy all they needed. Now, among the very poor who suffered was a woodcutter. He lived with his wife and two children, Hansel and Gretel, in a cottage on the edge of a great forest.

His wife was a strange woman with no love for her children at the best of times. And when there was scarcely any food to be shared around, she began wishing that something could happen to Hansel and Gretel.

"They are two extra mouths to feed," she told her husband, one night, after the children had gone upstairs to bed. "Why don't we take them into the forest in the morning and leave them there?"

The poor woodcutter was horrified at his wife's cruel words. But he was a weak man, secretly afraid of her, and when she raised her voice and began to shout, he buried his head in his hands.

"I tell you," she screamed, "This is what we must do. Why should I starve for their sake? Tomorrow we will rouse them at dawn and pretend we are taking them into the forest to gather brushwood."

In vain, the poor man tried to persuade his wife to change her mind. As they began to argue, their loud voices disturbed the children, and Hansel crept to the top of the stairs to listen. When at last he heard his father say, "Very well, wife, we

shall do as you say," he stole back to bed.

"Don't sob!" he whispered, putting his arm round Gretel's trembling shoulders. "It wasn't our father who wanted to send us into the forest."

"There are fierce wolves in the forest," Gretel sobbed, for she didn't have her brother's stout heart. "We shall never find our way home safely."

"Never mind about the wolves," her brother said cheerfully. "I've thought of a plan already!"

Hansel lay awake in his little bed until he heard his parents go upstairs. Then, as silent as a mouse, he slipped out of the room and stole down to the backdoor.

The big key squeaked in the lock as Hansel turned it and his heart pounded, but he was certain that he had waited long enough for his mother and father to be sound asleep.

How bright the silver moon was as Hansel ran into the little patch of garden at the back of their hut! It made the pebbles look like silver pennies as he began filling his pockets with them. As soon as his pockets were bulging, Hansel returned to the house, remembering to turn the big key so that his father would suspect nothing.

"You mustn't cry or look frightened," he warned his little sister, as they went down to breakfast the next morning.

Breakfast was just half a slice of stale bread and a glass of water. The children asking no questions when they saw their father shoulder his axe.

"We are taking you into the forest for an outing," their mother said. "We are

going into a strange part of the forest today where the brushwood will be more plentiful."

Soon they were on their way. For a time the woodcutter took a familiar path and then they went deeper into the forest and Hansel knew the moment had come to carry out his plan. As he lingered behind the others, he began dropping his white pebbles, one by one. No matter how far they journeyed into the dark forest, the pebbles would help him to find his way home again.

"Why do you keep falling behind, Hansel?" his mother shouted crossly.

"I was just trying to see if our little house was still visible through the trees," Hansel replied.

Poor little Gretel was beginning to grow very tired when, at last, the woodcutter rested his heavy axe against a tree and said, "Now children, help us to collect a few sticks. We'll make a fire and then you can sit by it while your mother and I go off to see what brushwood we can find."

Their father looked at them sadly when this was done. "Stay close to the fire," said he, "until our return."

"He doesn't mean to come back for us," Gretel whispered, as she watched him hurry after his wife.

"Perhaps he will come back," Hansel said. "Let's do as he says and wait here."

They waited until it was almost dark. Then Gretel curled up beside her brother and fell fast asleep. Hansel let her sleep. It would be much wiser to wait until the friendly moon was riding in the sky. Then he would be able to see his trail of pebbles by its silvery light.

When Gretel awoke the moon was already up but the forest looked different, so full of strange shapes, that she clung to Hansel,

"We are really lost now," she whimpered. "We'll never find our way home."

"Yes, we shall," said her brother, pulling her to her feet. "Help me find the first pebble."

In time it became a kind of game and Gretel was proud whenever she discovered a pebble before her brother. All through the rest of the night they walked, following their pebble trail until, just as it began to grow light, they saw their little house among the trees.

"We're home!" Hansel shouted joyfully, and taking Gretel's hand, he pulled her towards the hut.

Their father wept tears of happiness when he saw his children again for he was certain that by now they would have been devoured by wolves. But his wife frowned and would scarcely speak to them.

That night she said to her husband, "Well, they found their home this time. We should have taken them deeper into the forest."

It wasn't long before her loud voice roused Hansel, and he crept to the top of the stairs to listen.

"This time," he heard his mother say, "we'll start out earlier and make sure they don't find their way home."

Once again, Hansel put his plan into action. But, alas, when he crept down to the backdoor, he found it locked and the key removed.

"Don't worry," he said to Gretel, when he returned with empty pockets. "I couldn't get the pebbles, but bread will do as well. You must give me your slice at breakfast."

The very next morning, the woodcutter and his wife took Hansel and Gretel into the forest, and this time Hansel dropped crumbs of bread as he walked along. Just as before they told the children to wait by the fire for them when, at last, they reached a dark, lonely part of the forest.

"Don't go to sleep, Gretel!" Hansel urged his sister, when they found themselves alone. "It is nearly night time already and we must find the crumbs I dropped as fast as we can."

But, oh dear! What do you think had happened? The hungry little birds had eaten every morsel of the bread. Hansel refused to be downcast when he guessed the truth. "We'll walk and walk until we find the right path," he said bravely.

It was so dark and eerie in the forest that Gretel soon began to cry, and even her brother began to lose heart until, suddenly, a beautiful white bird appeared, fluttering from branch to branch. "It's just as if it was showing us the way to go," Hansel cried. "Let's follow it!"

The bird led them to a clearing in the forest and there, standing all by itself, was the most wonderful cake and gingerbread house you could ever imagine. The roof was made of gingerbread and pancakes and the walls of clear sugar. The window

frames were of gaily striped barley sugar.

Hansel and Gretel stared at the wonderful little house in amazement.

Then Gretel cried, "Oh, I'm so hungry, Hansel!" And she broke off some barley sugar. And Hansel broke off some of the sweet cake that served as steps.

Soon they were munching to their hearts' content while the little white bird watched them from its perch on the rooftop.

"I knew the beautiful white bird was our friend," said Hansel, at last, his mouth full of cake. "I wonder who lives inside?"

Now the wonderful gingerbread house belonged to a wicked old witch, and presently she came hobbling out on to the step, leaning on her crutch.

Hansel and Gretel were so frightened when they saw her watching them that they let their cake and barley sugar fall

to the ground. But the old witch spoke to them kindly. "Come in, children," she said, "I have even nicer things to eat inside my little house." And she opened the door wide so that they could see the table laid with bowls of nuts and apples and sugar buns.

So in they went and soon they were sitting down to a marvellous feast. Then the old witch showed them two little white beds where they could sleep for the night.

But, oh dear me! It was all very different in the morning. As soon as they opened their eyes, the old witch pounced on Hansel and dragged him away to a cage, which she kept in a dark shed.

Gretel screamed with fright, but the witch only laughed. "That white bird you followed," she told her, "was all part of my magic. So too is this house. I use it to catch little children. Your brother, Han-

46

sel, will be the first to go into my cooking pot, but I must first fatten him up.''

There were no more nuts and apples for Gretel now. The old witch made her do all the cleaning and sweeping, and she fed her on the scraps from her own meals. Hansel, however, had cream every day and sugar buns and chicken in rich sauce.

The witch waited impatiently for him to grow fat but being a true witch she could not see very well, so whenever she went into the dark shed, she asked Hansel to push his finger out of the cage.

"That brother of yours refuses to grow fat," she grumbled to Gretel. "His finger feels as thin as a chicken bone."

This is exactly what she *was* feeling for Hansel had found a way to trick the old witch; whenever she visited him, he pushed a chicken bone through the bars instead of his own finger.

Well, one morning the witch decided that she could wait no longer. "I'll eat him just as he is!" she told Gretel. "Now then, child, light the big oven."

Gretel begged for Hansel's life with tears in her eyes, but the wicked old woman chuckled and pushed her to one side. "It will soon be your turn," she croaked. "Now light that oven!"

"I–I don't know how," Gretel murmured, at last. "The door is too big and heavy. . . ."

The witch was so impatient to get on with her cooking that she pulled open the door herself and lit the oven.

After a while, she said, "Go to the oven and see if it is hot enough!"

Once again, Gretel shook her head. "I won't know when the oven is hot," she whispered. "I–I wouldn't be able to tell you!"

"Little fool!" grumbled the witch, and she hobbled over to the oven, pulled open the big heavy door and – and, my goodness me, timid little Gretel gave her a great big push!

Into the oven, went the wicked witch, head first, and Gretel slammed the door shut. Never before had she pushed anyone – but then it was to save Hansel! She soon found the witch's key, and in a trice was running as fast as she could to the shed where Hansel crouched in his cage.

"Hansel! Hansel!" she cried. "We are saved! The old witch is dead and I have the key to unlock the padlock."

How pleased Hansel was to escape! He hugged his sister, and together they went back to the old crone's house. On the way, Gretel told her brother about the rubies and diamonds and pearls she had seen, as she polished and dusted.

"It must be witch's treasure," she went on. "And she was a real witch, you know, for she had red eyes and she could hear even a leaf fall to the ground. . ."

"But she couldn't see very well," Hansel smiled. "And that was lucky for us or she would have eaten me up long ago!"

"If she *was* a real witch, we can help ourselves to her treasure," Gretel said, as she showed her brother the chests filled with precious stones.

"Of course, we can," said Hansel. And he filled his pockets with rubies and pearls, just as, long ago, he had filled them with pebbles. And Gretel, not to be outdone, took some of the shining diamonds and put them in the pocket of her apron.

Then, hand in hand, they left the gingerbread house, which never again would trap little lost children, and set out for home.

But where was home? As they began wandering through the forest, Hansel whistled to keep up his courage. But Gretel felt ever so brave as they walked along. At last, they came to a broad river which they must cross. "We shall have to get to the other side somehow," said she. "I don't see a bridge or a boat – but there is a white duck swimming there. Oh Hansel, I believe she might carry us across if I called her." And she began to sing,

> "*Little duck, little duck so white,*
> *There's not a bridge or a boat in sight.*
> *We'll be your friends for ever and ever*
> *If only you'll carry us over the river.*"

And the little duck came to the water's edge.

"Quick, let's climb on her back," Hansel exclaimed, "before she swims away."

"No, no," Gretel said gently. "If we both climb on to her back she will have a heavy burden to carry. You go first, Hansel! Then she can return for me."

So Hansel climbed on to the white duck's back and was carried across the broad river. The duck returned for Gretel, and she thanked the bird politely when she found herself safely on the far bank.

"How strange that we should come upon this river," Hansel said, "and a duck willing to take us across it. I'm sure we are going to find our way home quite quickly now."

Hansel was right. After a while, he began to recognise the trees and then, they found a path which they both knew would take them to their own cottage.

"Come on, Gretel, I'll race you!" Hansel suddenly shouted, as he saw smoke rising. "Our cottage is not far."

Away he ran and after him ran Gretel. Of course Hansel was at the door long before his sister, but he waited so that they could surprise their father together.

They found him all alone in the kitchen. And when the poor woodcutter saw his children framed in the doorway, he was sure their ghosts had come to haunt him.

Then Gretel rushed forward. "We're home, father!" she cried. "We are really and truly home."

The woodcutter was so happy that he could find no words to tell them of his joy. Hansel emptied his pockets and the rubies and pearls scattered on the bare wooden table. Then Gretel put her own little pile of diamonds beside the other precious stones.

"We're rich," Hansel cried. "You have no more worries, father. These jewels will buy us all the food we want."

Before their father could say anything, Gretel told him all about the witch and the white duck. And then their father told them that his wife had left for good.

"I thought I would never see you again," he said, and his eyes filled with tears. "The treasure you have brought me is nothing compared to having you, my own children, safely home."

And he took Hansel and Gretel in his arms and hugged them as if he would never let them go.

The Frog Prince

HERE WAS ONCE a young Princess who had bright golden hair, the colour of ripe corn, and eyes as blue as the sea on a summer day. Her father was a powerful King and he loved his daughter so much that he showered her with gifts.

Now among the precious and expensive toys and baubles this Princess possessed, there was one which gave her hours and hours of pleasure. This was her golden ball. No other Princess in the world had such a wonderful ball and the Princess took it with her whenever she went out walking in the woods that surrounded her father's castle.

One day, as she tossed the ball into the air it dropped back – not into her hands – but into a deep well that had stood there in the woods for a hundred years or more.

The Princess was at first angry when she saw her beautiful golden ball disappear down the well. Then she grew upset, weeping and stamping her little foot on the grass.

Running to the well, she almost overbalanced as she tried to peer down into its inky depths. At last she sank down besides it, sobbing loudly into a delicate lace handkerchief.

Presently a frog came out of the well. It was fat and ugly and the Princess shuddered as she looked at it, but before she could run away, the frog spoke. "What will you give me, Princess," it asked, "if I go back into the well and fetch your golden ball?"

"You mean – you mean you really could!" exclaimed the Princess, her tears forgotten. "Oh, if only you will! You shall have my little gold cross set with rubies and, if that does not please, you may take my gold crown that glitters in the sunshine."

"Such things are of no use to me," the frog said.

"I have a white pony and a carriage lined with pink velvet and the smallest green dog in the world and a golden bird that never stops talking," the Princess said breathlessly. "And – and you may have them all if only you will fetch my beautiful golden ball . . ."

"No," said the frog. "What would I do with a pony, and a carriage lined with pink velvet or, for that matter, with the smallest green dog in the world or a bird that forever talks?"

"Then what *do* you want?" demanded the Princess, pouting and stamping her foot.

"I want you to promise to take me back with you to your fine castle," said the frog. "I want you to permit me to feed from your own plate and sleep in your own bed."

The Princess looked at the frog in astonishment. Then she thought, "What a stupid old thing it is! I can promise that quite easily, here and now. Just let me get the ball – then we'll see . . ."

But her words were very different from her thoughts. "Oh, very well, frog," she said. "I'll take you home and you can eat from my plate and sleep in my bed. Yes, I promise!"

Satisfied, the frog hopped back into the

well and was soon back, holding the golden ball. The Princess bent down and snatched her precious toy. Then, without a word of thanks, she ran away through the trees.

"Wait! Wait for me!" the frog croaked. But the Princess did not even turn round. On and on she ran until she was safely inside her father's castle.

That night, as she sat down to dinner with her father and his courtiers, there was a knock on the door, which though not very loud was plainly heard by all who sat round the table.

"Go and see who it is," said the King, turning to his daughter, for he wished to prove to his courtiers that his daughter was still obedient even if spoilt.

Now the Princess knew quite well that she must obey her father when he spoke in a certain tone so she went to the door. She was soon back, however, her face pale and her eyes unusually bright. "It w—was n—nothing, father," she stammered. "It was nothing but the branch of a tree striking the door."

But no sooner had she begun to eat than the knocking came again and this time her father spoke more sternly. "Whoever is knocking must be allowed to enter," he ordered.

Can you guess what was outside the castle door? It was the frog come to claim its reward.

"No, father, don't send me to the door again," the Princess cried, blushing red and pretending to be very gay. "You can't imagine what a stupid ugly old frog I found out there on the step. If I open the door it is sure to follow me inside."

"What can a frog want with you?" asked the King.

"Well, I – I promised that it could come here when it fetched my beautiful golden ball out of the well," the Princess admitted. "And I said it could eat off my plate and sleep in my bed. But, father, it was just a way of getting back my golden ball."

"A promise given must be kept," said her father sternly. "Open the door, daughter."

The Princess had no choice then but to obey and in came the frog, hopping after her over the marble floor.

"Now, lift me up beside you," it said, when they reached the table.

The Princess hesitated, but her father told her to do what the frog asked, and all the courtiers, some fat and some thin, tittered behind their hands at the sight of a frog sitting beside the proud Princess.

"Now, push your little gold plate nearer so that we may eat together," said the frog. And the Princess did so, grudgingly.

The frog enjoyed the meal, but the Princess would not touch the food and, presently, watched by all who sat round the royal table, she pushed back her chair and said she was going to bed.

"Take me with you," said the frog, and the Princess, choking with rage and shame, took hold of the frog with two fingers and carried him to her room.

"Now put me in your bed between your sheets of silk," said the frog. And when the Princess obstinately shook her head, the frog added, "Or I will tell your father, the King."

"Hateful, horrid creature!" screamed the Princess. "I cannot bear the sight of you!" And losing her temper completely, she dashed the poor frog against the wall.

As the frog fell, it changed into a tall handsome young man with gentle eyes and a charming smile.

"Thank you, Princess," he said, holding out his hands towards her. "You alone had the power to save me from a wicked witch. Only a Princess with golden hair and eyes as blue as the sea, who would take me into her castle, could break the spell she cast upon me."

Of course, the Princess was ashamed that she had shown so little pity for the Prince when he was a frog. But the Prince took her in his arms, begging her to come away with him to his own Kingdom.

No one was happier than the King when he saw the happy pair together. Then, out of the woods, came a fine carriage drawn by four black horses with ostrich feathers on their heads and the Princess and her Frog Prince drove away to start a new and wonderful life together.

The Little Tin Soldier

ONCE UPON A TIME a little boy was given a box of tin soldiers for his birthday. He took them out of their long box and stood them up – all twenty-five of them – and how smart they looked in their blue and red uniforms and shining black boots.

"What's this?" he shouted suddenly. "One of my tin soldiers has only got one leg. What a shame!"

It was true. The twenty-fifth tin soldier had been made last of all out of an old tin spoon and there just wasn't enough lead to finish him off.

Stiff and proud stood the one-legged tin soldier at the end of the row. Even if he did only have one leg, he was still a soldier and he knew his place. There was a great deal to look at in the room, however, for it was quite crowded with birthday presents.

There was a jolly pink elephant and a Jack-in-the-box, who kept trying to attract attention by springing out. There were carved wooden animals and puppets-on-strings and a number of puzzles and books. But the best present of all was the castle. It was made out of cardboard, and it looked very real once the little boy had set it up on the table. There were tiny trees to place in the courtyard and a small lake, which was no more than a piece of glass, on which three graceful waxen swans could swim.

All the toys regarded this wonderful

castle with envy, but not the one-legged tin soldier who kept his eyes front, like all good soldiers should! Later on, that same afternoon, the boy came upon a little dancing girl – perhaps she really belonged to the castle, who knows? And he placed her in front of the castle. At the sight of the pretty dancing girl, the tin soldier no longer felt he could stand forever at attention, eyes front. She was so lovely with that flower in her shining hair and a ribbon of blue silk round her slender waist, to which a bright star was pinned.

Now, the little dancing girl who stood, poised on one leg with her arms out-stretched, was only made out of paper. The tin soldier knew nothing of that. To him, she was the most beautiful girl he had ever seen and, almost at once, he lost his heart to her.

"How graceful she is!" he told himself. "How dainty! There is nobody in the whole world I would rather marry."

For the first time, the little tin soldier began to regret that he lived in a box in company with twenty-four other soldiers who all looked exactly alike.

"That box is no place to take a lady

wife," he thought. "Supposing – supposing she did find me acceptable as a husband. I must do something about shifting my headquarters."

As the tin soldier stood lost in thought, the room became quite dark and presently the boy ran in to put all his toys away for the night.

"Can't – mustn't lose sight of her so soon," murmured the tin soldier, and he hopped on his one stout leg behind a musical box so that the boy wouldn't see him.

All toys have lives of their own after midnight and as soon as the big clock on the landing struck twelve, the birthday toys began moving about. The pink elephant was so clumsy that he knocked over Jack-in-the-box, who tried to pull his trunk, and there was soon quite a disturbance in the playroom. Only the little tin soldier remained still, his eyes fixed on the dancing girl.

Jack-in-the-box, a rude fellow at the best of times, teased the one-legged soldier about the dancing girl. "She won't want anything to do with you," he sneered. "A cat may look at a Queen but the Queen doesn't have to look at the cat!"

The tin soldier said nothing to this for it seemed that the beautiful girl was looking at him. She did not speak and she did not move but he was sure that she had noticed him. So he remained where he was, at attention, but with his eyes on the dancer.

Soon after breakfast the next morning, the boy rushed into the playroom. He took his twenty-four soldiers out of their box and stood them in a row. "One, two, three, four, five . . ." he began to count. There was one missing. Then he found the one-legged soldier behind the musical box. "I will put you by the window," he said. "You can do special guard duty on your own."

"That suits me very well," thought the tin soldier, as he found himself standing beside the open window. "I can still see the little lady."

The boy forgot about his soldier and began playing with his puzzles. It was not until he heard the window rattle and saw the curtains billow that he rushed over to save his toy from being blown away. Alas, he was too late. The wind carried the little tin soldier into the street and dropped him on the paving stones beneath the window.

The soldier was very frightened as he lay there but he did not shout for help as a civilian might have done. He kept his soldier-like bearing even in those dreadful circumstances.

The boy was upset at losing his toy. He ran down the stairs into the street to look for him but the tin soldier was lying in a crack between two paving stones and almost invisible. Then it began to rain and the boy went indoors and forgot all about his lost toy.

Presently, as the tin soldier lay there, two other boys came along. Their ragged coats were soaking wet but they didn't seem to mind. One of them stubbed his toe on the tin soldier and picked him up. "Look! A one-legged tin soldier!" he cried. "Let's make him a paper boat and sail him down the gutter."

Goodness me! The little soldier felt quite sea-sick as the swift-running water carried him on and on. His boat rocked up and down in a very alarming way and it took him all his time to keep his balance. But worse was to come. The water from the gutter flowed into a drain that was as

black as night.

This drain was the home of some very fierce rats and almost at once the rats were after him. "What right have you here?" they questioned him. "Show us your passport: Stop! Stop!" And they tried to grab the paper boat with their yellow teeth.

"This is the end," the tin soldier told himself. And he thought of his dancing lady and wished that she could see how bravely he was prepared to die. But before the rats could have their way, the swirling waters tossed the flimsy boat out of their reach and carried it forward. On and on, it sailed until it entered the deep and dangerous waters of a great canal.

Almost immediately it began to sink. The brave little soldier kept tight hold of his musket as the waters closed over his head.

Just at that very moment, a huge fish came swimming along. Did it take the tin soldier for some exotic dragonfly, I wonder? We shall never know. All we do know is that it swallowed him up, musket included!

How black it was inside that big fish! The little tin soldier needed all his courage to keep up his spirits. "I will die like a true soldier," he told himself, "standing at attention." But it was not easy to hold himself erect for the fish dived every now and then at great speed, and the tin soldier was tossed about like a cork.

After all, that monster fish had not long to live for it was caught by a fisherman. The fisherman, as was the custom, took his catch straight to the market-place, where, each day, the housewives gathered to buy their fish.

"Now, what is happening?" the little tin soldier asked himself, as suddenly he found everything very still. Of course, he had no way of guessing that the fish was now lying on a slab waiting to be sold. And it was not long before a woman came along and bought it.

Who do you think she was? I'll tell you – the little boy's mother. What a surprise for the little boy when he heard his mother calling him to come to the kitchen.

"Guess what I've found inside this fish," she said, as he ran to her. "Look, it's that one-legged tin soldier you lost out of the window!"

Then she took a wet cloth and carefully cleaned the soldier's uniform. "Now," said she, "he is almost as good as new. Take him and put him beside the others."

The little tin soldier was so happy to find himself in the presence of his dancing lady that he could scarcely stop himself from saluting her. Alas, he had not long to enjoy her company, for that same day one of the little boy's friends, in a fit of temper, snatched him up and threw him in the fire.

"I have escaped death so many times," the tin soldier thought, as the hot flames licked his face. "Why should I fear it now? At least I can die with my eyes fixed on my lady love."

But then, as his bright uniform began to melt, a gust of wind blew the dancing girl straight towards him. And the tin soldier stood to attention in a final salute as she joined him in the fire.

So that was the end of the tin soldier and the pretty dancing girl of the castle. Do you think it was a sad ending? Perhaps and perhaps not! When the boy's mother raked out the fire in the morning, she found, among the ashes, a lump of tin, shaped like a heart and beside it, so close that the two were touching, a tiny metal star, the very same the little lady had worn over her heart.

Jack and the Beanstalk

ONCE UPON A TIME there was a young boy called Jack. He was a lazy good-natured boy, content to stay at home and help his widowed mother in the garden and with the milking.

It is true that they had only one cow, but she was the best milker for miles around and Jack was very fond of her.

"I don't know what we would do without Daisy-Bell," his mother would often say, "for times are hard and without her milk we would go hungry."

The day came, alas, when the widow found she had not enough money to pay the rent for their tiny cottage.

There's nothing left to sell," she told Jack, "but the cow. You will have to take her into market this morning and see how much you can get for her."

Jack began to argue with his mother, but when he saw that her mind was made up, he said, "Don't worry, mother. I'll take Daisy-Bell to market and, you'll see, I'll strike a hard bargain." And off he went.

Not even the thought of selling his

beloved cow could keep Jack unhappy for very long. And soon he was whistling cheerfully as he drove Daisy-Bell along the road. As he walked behind her, he was suddenly surprised to come upon a stout little man seated on a pile of stones on the grass verge.

"Good-day to you," said the stranger. "Where are you going on such a fine day?"

"To market to sell my cow," said Jack, very pleased to have an excuse for stopping. "She's a fine cow and I mean to get a good price for her."

"I tell you what," said the little man. "Take these in exchange for your cow. I like the look of you and will do you a favour."

"A favour!" Jack exclaimed in disgust, as he stared down at the five brightly coloured beans the stranger had put into his hand. "Beans for Daisy-Bell!"

"They're magic," replied the stranger. "Plant them tonight and see what happens."

At the word 'magic', Jack pricked up his ears. Finally, he put the beans in his pocket and the little man took the cow.

Poor Jack – what trouble he met when he arrived back home with the beans. His mother screamed and wept in turns until Jack could stand it no longer. He planted the beans and then went, supperless, to bed.

But, goodness me! These beans *were* magic for in the morning the first thing Jack saw was an enormous beanstalk outside the cottage. "I'll climb that!" he decided. And, without a word to his mother, he began to climb. Up, up, up he went, not daring to look downwards.

The beanstalk stretched ahead of him endlessly, like a ladder, into the clouds. Gritting his teeth, Jack kept on climbing until, suddenly, he found he could jump from the beanstalk on to firm ground. Though he didn't know it, he was in the country of the giants!

"I can't turn back now," Jack told himself, and he set off down a broad white road which led him eventually to a huge castle.

Now Jack had not eaten any breakfast and the smell of roast meat coming from the kitchen was very tempting. He ran to the door and boldly knocked. "Can you spare me a bite to eat, ma'am," he asked, smiling up at the tall woman who answered his knock.

"You can't come in," the woman said, in a frightened voice. "Poor boy, you have come to a giant's castle. It's fortunate that my husband is out at the moment."

"I'm not afraid of giants," said Jack bravely, "but I am ever so hungry."

Now the giant's wife had a very kind heart and what's more she was lonely.

"Very well," she said at last. "But you can't stay. My husband would almost certainly want to eat you if ever he set eyes on you."

Just as Jack was telling her all about Daisy-Bell, the castle began to shake as if caught up in an earthquake, and the giant's wife whispered, "Hide! It's my husband come home!" She pushed Jack behind a huge barrel and begged him to keep quiet. Then she ran to the oven and brought out a roast hog and other dainties, which she placed on the table.

As the giant strode into the room, Jack peeped out from behind the barrel. "So that's what a giant looks like," he thought. "My, he could finish me off with two

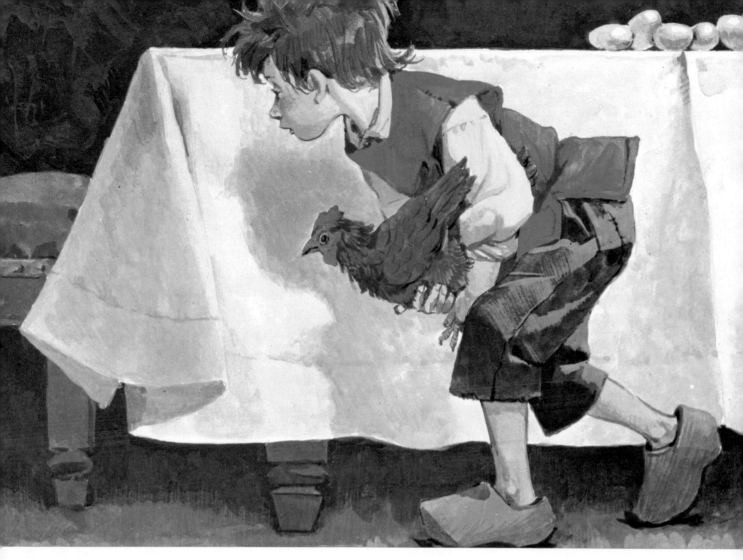

bites, I do declare."

The giant's wife fussed around her husband until he had eaten. Then she brought him his sacks of gold which usually put him in a good humour.

Presently the giant grew tired of counting his gold and, putting his great head on the table, fell fast asleep.

Jack waited a moment, then he crept out of his hiding-place, took the sacks filled with gold and ran from the castle. Down the beanstalk he climbed, so excited that he began shouting for his mother long before he reached the bottom.

The widow, as she heard his story, begged her son to be content with the gold. But Jack would not promise to put an end to his adventures so quickly.

Not long afterwards, he climbed the beanstalk again and presented himself at the giant's castle. This time, the giant's wife was not very pleased to see him but she asked him in for a brief visit. As they talked, her husband's heavy step was heard and, pushing Jack into a cupboard, she took a roast ox out of the oven and set it on the table.

The giant sniffed suspiciously as he sat down, "Fee-fi-fo-fum, I smell the blood of an Englishman . . ." he roared. "Be he alive . . ."

"You smell nothing but my roast," said his wife quickly. And her husband nodded and began to eat. Then he called for his magic hen, which laid eggs of solid gold.

Jack watched the golden eggs drop on to the table and, presently, as the giant

63

dozed off, he crept out of his hiding place and snatched the wonderful hen.

As Jack fled from the castle, the hen began to squawk so loudly that the giant awoke. He missed his magic bird at once and with a mighty roar thundered out of the kitchen to look for the thief.

But Jack had a good start. Breathless and still clutching the squawking hen, he reached the beanstalk and clambered down to safety. Now, he had the giant's gold and the giant's magic hen, but still he longed to try his luck a third time.

Early one morning, he climbed the beanstalk again, promising himself that this would be his last adventure. When he reached the castle, he made no attempt to find the giant's wife, feeling sure she would refuse to let him in. Instead, he entered by a small window and soon found his way to the vast kitchen. Then diving into the nearest hiding-place, which happened to be the oven, he watched through a crack.

When the castle began to rock, he knew the giant was coming and presently he strode into the room. His wife hurriedly set out cold slices of meat, as thick as logs, on the table. Her husband sniffed at them and then looked about him. "Fee-fi-fo fum," he suddenly roared, "I smell the blood of an Englishman. Be he alive or be he dead, I'll grind his bones to make my bread!"

His wife trembled at these terrible words but her conscience was clear. "What nonsense, husband!" she said. "I expect you're remembering the roast you had yesterday."

Then she persuaded the giant to sit

down at the table and begin his meal. After he had eaten, her husband called loudly for his magic harp and his wife ran to get it for him.

Jack shivered with excitement as he saw the giant place the harp on the table and heard him say, "Now, play for me!"

In an instant, the kitchen was filled with the sweetest music imaginable. As he listened Jack vowed to himself that he would have the magic harp, come what may. When the harp began to play a gentle lullaby, he saw the huge head begin to nod and soon the giant's snores were louder than the music. This was the moment young Jack had been waiting for and he jumped out of the oven and crept over to the table.

The harp was much easier to carry than the struggling, squawking hen but it, too, had a voice. And, as Jack ran from the castle, it called out, "Master! Master!"

Up struggled the giant and half-asleep he groped for the door. Once outside, he let out a mighty roar as he spied Jack.

What a chase that was! If the giant hadn't stumbled over his own big feet, he would have had the boy by the hair. As it was, Jack reached the beanstalk first and down he scrambled, as nimble as a squirrel. After him came the giant!

"Mother, mother throw me the axe," Jack shouted, as he reached the ground. And snatching it up, he chopped away at the beanstalk until, with a mighty crash, it fell to the ground. So did the giant, and he disappeared down the enormous hole he made and was never again seen.

As for Jack and his mother, they had the gold and the magic hen and best of all, the harp, to keep them happy for the rest of their days.

The Ugly Duckling

ONCE UPON A TIME, in the quietest part of the woods, a mother duck was sitting on her eggs. Never had the countryside looked more beautiful for it was summer and the grass and trees were fresh and green. But Mother Duck wasn't enjoying the warm sunshine. She was lonely and she was tired.

"How much longer will it be?" she kept asking herself, as she waited for the welcome sound of the little raps that would tell her the ducklings were ready to burst out of their shells.

Then, oh then, the first of the eggs cracked open and out tumbled a pretty little yellow duckling with a feeble, "Peep! Peep!"

Mother Duck was delighted. "Quack! Quack!" she said, in greeting. And she knew her long weary wait was at an end for, almost at once, her first duckling was joined by five more, all just as pretty.

What a proud mother she was! "I'll parade them in the poultry-yard," she told herself. "Quack! Quack!" she said aloud. "You little darlings!"

Mother Duck's joy was short-lived when she looked behind her. There was still another egg in the nest. Goodness, how big it was! Much bigger than any of her others. "I do hope it isn't a turkey's egg," she thought, as she sat down again. "Oh dear, it's very hard being a mother these days!"

When the big egg finally cracked open, poor Mother Duck looked at her last born with surprised dismay. What sort of a child

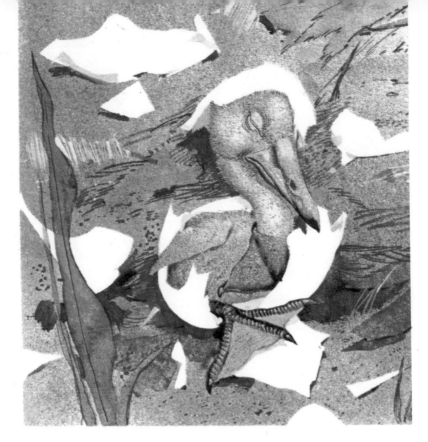

was this ugly grey-feathered little monster?

"Quack! Quack!" she cried in alarm. "What are you? I hope you're not a turkey child. I just couldn't bear that kind of disappointment."

"Peep! Peep!" said her other little children, as they greeted their new brother. "Why aren't you pretty like us? What makes you so ugly?"

"He may not be one of us," said Mother Duck. "We shall soon find out when I take you to the pond for your first swimming lesson. If he is a turkey child, by any chance, then you may be sure he won't be able to swim."

The Ugly Duckling, as he heard this, remained silent. The unhappy feeling he was beginning to have spread all over him like a damp mist.

"Am I really so different?" he asked himself. "Can I be as ugly as they say?"

But Mother Duck knew her duties as a mother. "I shall have to show you off to the Grand Duchess," she told her new family. "Then you will be accepted in the poultry-yard." And she stared particularly hard at her youngest, adding, "Poor little monster! It's not your fault, I suppose. I'll take care of you as long as I can . . ."

"How big and wide the world is!" said the duckling, who had been born first. "Is this all of it?"

"Of course not," said their mother. "There is the poultry-yard, and the field. But first I must take you to the pond. Then we shall see how well you take to the water." And once again she looked hard at the Ugly Duckling.

As Mother Duck set off for the pond, she met one of her most trusted friends, an old Duck who always believed in speaking her mind.

"If I were you," said the old Duck, when her eyes lighted on the Ugly Duckling, I would hide him away in the woods. He does you no credit, no credit at all."

But Mother Duck did not agree. "We shall see if he can swim," she said, and she

called her family to follow her to the pond. On their arrival, in she dived and splash! In jumped her children.

Mother Duck watched them proudly. She could see at once that they were going to be excellent swimmers – even the ugly one could swim like an expert.

"He can't be a turkey child after all," she told herself. "He's swimming even better than the others." And she began to feel quite proud of him.

But, oh dear, where were the loud quacks of approval she was expecting from her friends? They weren't watching her

pretty ones. No, their beady eyes were fixed on her youngest and they were mocking him with loud harsh cackles of jeering laughter.

Mother Duck wanted to dive to the bottom of the pond with shame as she heard the insults hurled at her son.

"Monster!", sneered one big drake. "Freak – ugly freak!" shouted another. "Take him to the Grand Duchess. Let her pass sentence on him."

The Grand Duchess had ruled over the poultry-yard for ten years or more and her word was law. "He is not one of us," said she. "He can only bring disgrace on our proud family."

Well, that was the beginning of terrible days for the Ugly Duckling. He was teased, chased, bitten and pecked. Even his own brothers and sisters turned against him, refusing to let him play in their games.

"I will run away," he decided at last. "I am not wanted here and if I stay I will only be pecked to death."

Sad to say, no one missed the Ugly Duckling as he left the poultry-yard and set out to find happiness in the wide, wide world. He walked for a long time until he came to some wild, lonely marsh-lands. "I won't expect to make any friends," he thought. "I'm too ugly for that, and it's lonely enough here for me to stay without troubling anyone."

But that night, as he settled down among the reeds, two wild geese came upon him, and the Ugly Duckling asked very humbly if they would keep him company.

"You're far too ugly to expect any friendship from us," they told him. "But we won't drive you away."

Early the next morning, as the two proud young geese rose into the air, there was a sudden deafening, "Bang! Bang!" And they dropped out of the sky like two stones.

Trembling with fright, the Ugly Duckling stayed in his hiding-place among the reeds until the huntsman's dogs came sniffing round. But they had no interest in such a bedraggled creature as the duckling and left him where he lay.

"Heavens!" the Ugly Duckling told himself, "I'm even too ugly for the dogs; they couldn't bear to touch me!" And he got up and began to run from that terrible place.

On and on he went, not daring to stop or look round until, late that same day, he came upon a tumbled-down old hut, whose broken door was swinging this way and that in the cold wind.

Shivering and weak with hunger, the Ugly Duckling saw that he could just manage to squeeze through the open door and so get into the hut. Not caring much what happened to him, he slipped into the dark room.

Now, an old woman lived in this ramshackled old place, with her cat and her hen. And when she saw the Ugly Duckling she made him welcome.

"You can lay me a nice fresh egg for my breakfast each morning," said she, as she peered down at the duckling. But being very short-sighted, she had no idea what a foolish command that would turn out to be!

As the weeks went by and the duckling produced no eggs, the old woman grew impatient with him, often chasing him out of the hut into the bitterly cold winds of autumn. And, following the example of their mistress, the cat and hen no longer pretended to care about him.

"Of what use are you here?" demanded the cat, one day. "Can you purr? Can you arch your back and give out sparks like me?"

"No," said the Ugly Duckling timidly. "I can't do any of these things."

"Can you cluck and lay eggs?" teased the hen.

"No," admitted the Ugly Duckling. "I can't cluck and I can't lay eggs."

At this, the hen scratched the ground and glared fiercely down on the poor duckling and the cat showed its teeth and chased him out of the hut. "Don't ever dare to come back," it hissed.

70

Now came the hardest time of all for the Ugly Duckling. A cruel frost held the whole countryside in its grip. The trees in the woods were white ghosts; the ground was hard, like iron, and the bare hedgerows under which he tried to creep, would not give him shelter.

With nowhere to go and not a soul to speak to, the Ugly Duckling could only wander on and on. Too weak to be able to fly, he thought of the pond at the farm where he had pleased his mother by swimming so well.

He began to long to find water and when at last he came upon a small pool that was not yet frozen over, he dragged himself into the water. But he had to keep swimming, round and round, as the ice slowly formed. And soon he found he was its prisoner.

"I am going to die," the Ugly Duckling thought, as he felt himself held fast in the icy grip.

Certainly, the duckling would have died if a farmer on his way home had not spotted the bird. He broke the ice with his heavy boot and freed the bedraggled bird. Then he carried it to the farm.

The farmer's children were thrilled to have a wild bird of their own. They thawed out the duckling before the fire, and gave him something to eat. When he grew stronger, they wanted to play with him.

Shrieking with laughter, they began chasing the Ugly Duckling round and round the huge kitchen until he thought his last hour had come.

In his terror, he flew straight into the milk churn and the milk slopped all over the newly washed floor. Then he fell into the butter-tub, and the farmer's wife lost her temper and began hitting out at him with her broom. His terror gave the Ugly Duckling fresh strength and with a desperate flapping of his wings he made for the open door and escaped.

For the rest of the long hard winter, he hid away in the woods, desperately weak but somehow managing to stay alive.

Then, one day, he looked up into the trees and saw that they were fresh and green. He felt the sun warming his wings and heard the birds, circling overhead, sing to each other of – Spring.

The winter was over at last and the Ugly Duckling began to try out his wings. He found he could fly and he rose into the air rejoicing in his new freedom.

Away he flew, over the trees and over the meadows until he saw below him a great royal park with a wide lake. And there, gliding over the water, were the most beautiful birds he had ever seen.

"How lovely they are," he thought wistfully. "Oh, if only I had been born to look like them!" And he dropped down on to the lake, determined to speak to them even if it should cost him his life.

As he swam towards the white birds, the Ugly Duckling bent his head and saw his image in the clear water. But what did he see? Not the ugly scarecrow that he expected – but a graceful, long-necked white swan!

"Welcome, brother," said the largest of the swans gliding up to him. "You may stay here for you are one of us!"

The Ugly Duckling knew then for the first time what it was to be happy. His happiness was so real and so deep that he forgot all the misery of his past life. And as the warm, friendly sun kissed his beautiful white feathers, the new swan took his place among his brothers. He had found his true family at last.

Rapunzel

ONG, LONG AGO there was once a witch who came to live in a certain village. She was a proper witch with a number of evil spells at her command, and the villagers were naturally terrified of her. They were also very sorry for the young couple who were her next-door-neighbours.

"Imagine living next door to a witch!" they whispered to each other, whenever they caught sight of the young wife. "And to think she is going to have a baby!"

One day, as the young wife sat at her window looking down on the witch's fine herb garden, a great longing swept over her for a particular herb, called rampion, which she saw growing there.

"I shall die if I can't have it," she told her husband, that night.

"Only the witch grows that purple herb,"

said her husband, turning pale.

"Then you must ask her for some," replied his wife calmly.

Now to approach the witch was quite beyond his courage so, that night, he scaled the high wall, jumped down into the witch's garden and helped himself to the precious herb.

His wife ate the rampion eagerly and the next night asked for more. "I shall die," said she, "if I don't get it."

Trusting that his luck would hold, the young man once again entered the witch's garden, but this time the witch herself was waiting for him.

"Take all the rampion you want," she croaked, with a spiteful leer, "but give me your promise that I shall have your first born child for myself."

Terrified that she would turn him into a scorpion or a spider, the poor man gave his promise and escaped over the wall.

When he told his wife all that had happened, she refused to be down-hearted.

"What would an old crone do with a baby!" she laughed. "No, no, she won't bother us if we don't bother her!"

But the wife was wrong. A day or two after her baby girl was born, the witch suddenly appeared, snatched the child from its cradle and vanished.

Now the old witch really did want a child of her own. She named the baby Rapunzel, after the herb, and brought her up in the loneliest part of a deep forest. When she was twelve, others say somewhat older, Rapunzel was so lovely that the witch grew fiercely jealous of her beauty.

"No man must ever set eyes on her," she told herself and, using her magic, she conjured up a tall tower in which she placed Rapunzel.

There was no entrance to this tower except by a window at the very top. And whenever the enchantress wished to see Rapunzel, she stood at the bottom and called, "Rapunzel, Rapunzel, let down your hair!" And the girl would come to the window and throw down her long golden hair which served the old witch as a ladder.

One day, a handsome young Prince came riding through the forest. He heard the witch's words and, dismounting from his horse, he watched unseen, as she climbed up until she reached the window.

The Prince waited until he saw the old crone leave the tower by means of the long golden hair and then vanish into the forest. He was loath to mount his horse and ride away and when he heard sweet singing coming from the high little window, he was more than ever resolved to enter the mysterious tower.

The very next night, when it was growing dark, the Prince returned and, after the manner of the witch, called out, "Rapunzel, Rapunzel let down your hair!" Down came the long braid, as fine as spun gold, and grasping it eagerly, he began to climb. But the greeting the young man received from the lovely young girl was far from flattering. Never having seen a man in her life, Rapunzel shrank away from him in terror.

"There is nothing to be afraid of," said the Prince, and he spoke so gently that Rapunzel permitted him to take her hand. Soon they were talking as if they had known each other all their lives. "I will come to you each night," the young man promised, "and one day you will leave this place to become my wife."

"You must bring me skeins of silk so that I can weave a rope," Rapunzel told him. "That is the only way I can escape."

The Prince, after that first visit, paid many others and with each he produced a skein of silk so that Rapunzel could weave the long rope that would help her to escape to freedom. The witch suspected nothing until one dreadful day, as she sat talking to the girl, Rapunzel said dreamily, "Tell me, old Dame, why do you take so much longer to climb than my Prince?"

Her rage was terrible to see at these words, and then she brought out a pair of scissors and cut off Rapunzel's long golden plaits, before carrying her off to a lonely valley that lay hidden between mountains.

Returning to the room in the tower, the enchantress sat down to wait for the Prince. He came at last, calling out, "Rapunzel, Rapunzel let down your hair!"

The witch wound the shorn plaits around a hook and the poor Prince climbed upwards into the room. He was brave, but the sight of the wicked witch, her claw-like hands ready to scratch his face so startled him that he fell backwards out of the window.

Down, down, down he fell, landing in the midst of a thorn bush whose cruel thorns pierced his eyes.

No longer able to see, the blind Prince wandered through the forest and then out into the countryside. Fearing that he had lost Rapunzel forever, he became no better than a beggar, living on alms as he moved from one place to the next. A whole year passed and then one day he came to the lonely valley between two mountains where the witch had hidden Rapunzel.

Are you surprised that Rapunzel should remember him? Or that her warm loving tears should fall upon his poor sightless eyes and make him see again! Well, that is truly what happened, and the wicked witch could do nothing about it! You see, against true, lasting love, she had no powers at all! So the Prince married Rapunzel and they both lived happily ever afterwards.

The Sleeping Beauty

THERE WAS ONCE a King and Queen who had everything in the world to make them happy except a child of their very own. Imagine their joy when, after years of waiting and hoping, the Queen gave birth to a beautiful baby daughter.

"We must share our happiness with all our friends!" exclaimed the happy Queen. "Our little daughter shall have a grand Christening Party."

Now, living in the realm were seven good fairies and they were among the first to receive their invitations to the christening.

"Let us give each of the fairies something they will always treasure," the Queen suggested, as she discussed the arrangements with her husband.

"I have already thought of that," replied the King. "At this very moment seven golden caskets, each containing a knife and fork studded with diamonds and rubies, are being made for them."

On the day of the Christening Party the guests were shown into the magnificent banqueting hall where a long table was laid with silver and gold dishes and sparkling crystal. The seven good fairies were seated at the top of the table and each fairy had a golden casket placed before her.

The banquet had scarcely begun when, all at once, an ancient fairy, whose face was wrinkled and yellow with age, entered the hall.

"I see no special place laid for me," she croaked in a voice so menacing that a hush fell upon the guests. And she pointed an accusing finger at the gold caskets. "Where is my casket?"

"No great harm is done," the King said quickly, as he saw his wife grow deathly pale. "Another place for you at table can easily be made."

But the ancient fairy would not be placated for with the best will in the world the King could not produce a casket for her.

When it was time for the good fairies to bestow their gifts upon the little Princess, the first fairy said, "She will be as lovely as a flower."

And the second said, "She will grow up full of sweetness and grace."

"She will dance divinely," said the third.

"And sing like a nightingale," said the fourth.

"She will master every musical instrument," decreed the fifth. And the sixth fairy said, "She will do everything to perfection."

Now it was the turn of the ancient fairy, for the seventh and the youngest of the good fairies held back, hoping that she might undo any spiteful wish the old crone might make.

"She will die when she pricks her finger

with a spindle," croaked the wicked fairy, as she stood over the sleeping child.

The stricken Queen swayed and almost fainted at these terrible words. Then the youngest fairy stepped forward.

"Take comfort, Your Majesties!" she cried. "The Princess will not die. She will fall into a sleep which will endure for one hundred years. At the end of that time a king's son will come and waken her."

The royal couple took comfort from the fairy's words and before the day was over, the King passed a law which decreed that all spinning wheels must be destroyed. Any person found using a spindle would be put to death.

When the Princess was about fifteen or sixteen years old, her parents took her to their castle in the country where she was free to roam the gardens with her little spaniel at her heels. Now it chanced that on a day when the sky was heavy with rain clouds, the young Princess decided to explore the castle itself, and she climbed the long winding stairs that led high up into the turret rooms. It was there, far removed from the tumult of the court, that she came upon an old woman bent over a large wooden wheel.

"What are you doing, mother?" the Princess asked curiously.

"I am spinning, child," replied the old dame, who had never heard of the King's law concerning spinning wheels.

"Spinning?" questioned the girl. "That's a new word. What fun! Do let me try."

Alas, as she took hold of the spindle the sharp needle pricked her finger and she fell to the ground. Thinking she was dead, the old spinster began calling loudly for help, and servants carried the Princess down the long stairs into the Queen's room.

"All that the wicked fairy prophesied has come to pass!" sobbed the broken-hearted Queen, as she gazed down on her child. "We must send for our good fairy and seek her advice."

So the King despatched his special messenger, a dwarf in seven league boots, to the farthest corner of his kingdom, and the good fairy set off immediately in her chariot drawn by two fiery dragons.

"My power cannot over-rule the power of the ancient fairy," said she, "but this much I can do. All living things in this castle will fall into a sleep that will last one hundred years. When your daughter awakes she will thus find everything as it is now."

The good fairy acted swiftly on her words. A touch of her wand and the fat food-taster slept in the very act of tasting the soup; the scullery maid fell asleep beside her pail and brush; the page boy slept as he teased the cat and the cat itself fell fast asleep. So too did all the horses in their stables and the chickens as they pecked at the corn.

Then the King and Queen kissed their daughter for the last time as she lay on her rich velvet couch, with her favourite pet asleep at her side.

As they rode sadly away, the fairy raised a great broad hedge of tangled thorny bushes all around the castle so that no one would discover the Sleeping Beauty who lay within.

Many a legend grew up around the

silent castle over the years, and many a gallant youth attempted to break through the thorn and brier. But all failed.

One day – it was a hundred years to the very hour when the Princess fell into her trance – a King's son came riding through the forest on his white horse.

At the sight of the grey castle so strangely protected by its jungle of bushes and brambles, the young Prince reined in his horse. "Tell me," said he, to an old peasant, as he gathered mushrooms nearby, "who lives in that silent mysterious castle?"

"No one rightly knows, sire," replied the old man, touching his cap. "Some say it is the home of a terrible ogre but others tell a different tale. When we were children, my grandfather amused us with the story of a Princess, a Sleeping Beauty, you might say, who fell under the enchantment of a wicked fairy. But that might well be a story told to children, who knows?"

"This is an adventure after my own heart," cried the dashing young Prince. "A Sleeping Beauty, you say? Well, let me be the first to find out the truth of it."

"Many have tried!" the old man warned. But the Prince paid no heed to his words as he rode forward, with sword drawn.

To his amazement, the thorny bushes parted before him as he advanced and, with no more than a scratch or two, he presently found himself in the huge court-yard of the castle itself.

What a strange sight met his eyes as he gazed about him! In their stalls, magnificent horses stood motionless and, beside them, their grooms sprawled on the ground, fast asleep. A cat slept with a little mouse an inch or two from its out-stretched paw and the mouse too was fast asleep. Dogs lay sleeping on the steps. Nothing stirred.

Even stranger was the sight of page boys, ladies-in-waiting and kitchen-maids, carved as if out of stone in the halls and passages of the castle. The young Prince wandered from room to room, astonished and fearful at the power of the enchantment that held the castle in its grip.

He came, at last, to the room where a girl, so beautiful that he caught his breath, lay fast asleep on a couch. The Prince tiptoed into the room and for a long moment was content to stand gazing down at the sleeping girl with her pet dog cuddled up beside her.

"Surely this must be my Sleeping Beauty!" he told himself. "How lovely she is!" And, greatly daring, he bent over and kissed her pale cheek.

The Princess stirred and opened her eyes. The fairy had made good her promise, for as the girl moved, the spaniel barked and jumped down from the royal bed.

"You have been such a very long time in coming," whispered the Princess softly, as she sat up.

And the King's son was enraptured. He knew nothing of the good fairy's powers or how, in her wisdom, she had decreed that a Prince should not only find the Princess but fall deeply in love with her!

As they talked to each other in low voices, after the manner of lovers, the whole castle came noisily to life. The food-taster, raising the ladle to his lips, wondered why the soup had turned stone cold. The scullery-maid, picked up her scrubbing brush and the naughty page pulled the cat's tail.

Out in the courtyard, horses stamped and neighed; the mouse made a dash for a convenient hole, and the hens began pecking hungrily at the corn.

Then the Princess took the Prince on a tour of the castle and nothing seemed strange or out of place to her.

In the kitchen the chêf was putting the final touches to the venison pie he had prepared a hundred years ago. And the Princess smiled her approval for it was her favourite dish.

The mistress of the linen chests begged her to inspect the sheets and fine lawn pillowcases trimmed with lace which was as white as the day, a hundred years ago, it had been made.

The good fairy had done her work with the utmost thoroughness. The Princess, as she went from room to room, saw nothing to alarm her or take away the happiness in her eyes as she clung to the Prince's arm.

And all those who served her had not the faintest inkling that they had been asleep for a hundred years. Nor did they ask questions concerning the handsome young man who has stolen their mistress's heart. It was enough to see the gentle smile that played about her lips as she walked at his side.

But to the Prince everything was very odd. For the world and fashion had moved on, and the dress and manner of all those he met belonged to an age long past.

"Let us marry here in the castle," said he, when the tour of inspection was over. "There is nothing I should like better."

And he held fast to the Princess's hand, as if afraid she would vanish.

"There is nothing I should like better than to be your wife," replied the lovely

Princess. "The chaplain shall marry us tomorrow."

Thus it was that the handsome King's son and the beautiful girl, who had slept for a hundred years, were married. Never had the Princess looked more beautiful for she wore the most gorgeous of her gowns. And if that, too, was a hundred years out of fashion, wisely, the Prince decided to make no comment.

Those who heard the story of The Sleeping Beauty came from far and wide to gaze upon the castle. Many returned home without believing a single word of it for – instead of the thorn and brier they expected to see – flowers and sweet-scented lavender bloomed everywhere, in and around the castle walls.

The Three Little Pigs

ONCE UPON A TIME there were three little pigs. "We would like to go out into the wide, wide world," they said to old Mother Sow, one day. "And see what it is like for ourselves."

"You do that!" said Mother Sow. And off they went.

But the world wasn't quite as nice as they had expected. The world had nasty wet rain that made them uncomfortable, and biting cold winds that made them

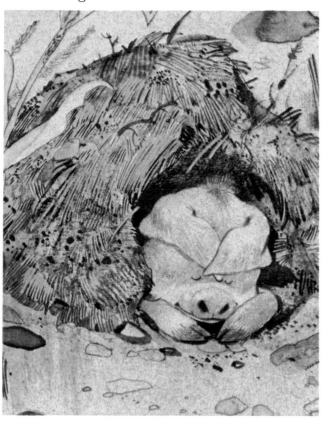

shiver, and quite soon the three little pigs began to wish they were home again.

"I'm going to build myself a proper house," said the first little pig.

"So am I," said the second little pig.

"Me too!" said the third little pig, who was by far the smartest of the brothers.

As they walked along the road, they saw coming towards them a man with a bundle of straw.

"Give me some of your straw," said the first little pig, "so that I can build myself a house."

The man willingly gave the little pig some of his straw and the little pig built himself a house. It fitted all around him so snugly that he had to squeeze himself through the door, but he didn't mind about that.

Now a big hungry wolf lived in the woods near by and he soon sniffed out the little pig. That night he paid him a visit. "Little pig, little pig, let me come in," he called out. But the little pig recognised the wolf's gruff voice.

"No, no, by the hair of my chinny chin chin," he called back.

"Then I'll huff and I'll puff and I'll blow your house in," said the wolf. And he huffed and he puffed and he did blow the house in. But the first little pig ran away too fast for the wolf to catch him.

Meanwhile, the second little pig had met a man with some bundles of sticks.

"Let me have some of your sticks," said

he. "I would like to build a house."

This, the man did most willingly, and the second little pig began to build himself a house. Half way through, he went inside and fell fast asleep, as you can see from the picture. It was just as well the big bad wolf didn't sniff him out until the next day when the house was finished.

"Little pig, little pig, let me come in," said the wolf, as he stood outside.

But the second little pig knew him by his gruff voice, and replied, "No, no, by the hair of my chinny chin chin."

So then the wolf huffed and he puffed and he blew the stick house to pieces. But the little pig ran away so fast that he escaped.

Now the third and smartest of the three little pigs decided to have a really strong house and so he built his house of good red bricks, for he wanted it to last for ever. He worked very hard on his house. But when it was finished, it had a stout green door and a proper tall chimney.

No sooner was he comfortably settled than his two little brothers came knocking at his door.

"That wicked wolf huffed and he puffed and he blew in my straw house," said the first little pig.

"And he huffed and he puffed and he blew away my stick house," said the second little pig."

"You're welcome to stay here," said the third little pig, "If you promise to take equal shares of the cleaning."

"We promise," said the two little pigs, in one voice. And they ran inside and slammed the big strong door.

The wolf, of course, was not very far away for now the scent of fat little pigs was stronger than ever. And oh how hungry it made him feel. He was so hungry that he couldn't wait until nightfall to pay the three little pigs a visit. Instead he went in the afternoon.

"Little pigs, little pigs, let me come in," said he, in his softest voice.

"No, no, by the hair of my chinny chin chin," called out the third little pig.

"Then I'll huff and I'll puff and I'll blow your house in," snarled the wolf.

And he did huff and puff but he could *not* blow in that strong brick house. When huffing and puffing wouldn't shift the little house, he began pushing and pushing it, and the three little pigs stood on chairs and watched him.

"I built my house of bricks," said the third little pig proudly. "That silly old wolf can't blow it away and he can't push it down."

Then the three little pigs sat down to afternoon tea while the wolf went back into the woods to think of another way to catch the little pigs.

The wolf spent a long time in the woods thinking out a plan. He wasn't very clever and all the thinking gave him a bad headache, but at last he *did* think of a way to trap the three little pigs.

"If I tell them I know where the finest turnips in the world can be found," he thought, "they will come out of that

strong little house of theirs and I'll be waiting for them."

So the next day, off he went to call on the three little pigs.

"Little pigs, little pigs," he called through the keyhole. "I've come to do you a big favour. Meet me at six tomorrow morning and I'll take you to the best field of turnips you've ever seen."

"I'll be ready for you," answered the third little pig.

That day, the third little pig made some enquiries about turnips, and soon learned for himself where they were to be found. And instead of meeting the wolf at six the next morning, he got up a whole hour earlier. Off he went with his basket and was soon home with three delicious, outsize turnips.

The wolf came along at six. He waited and he waited and he waited. And then, with his tail between his legs, he slunk off to work out another way of catching the little pigs.

Half way through the morning, he remembered the apple orchard. He had been there himself once or twice, but a wolf has to be very hungry indeed to eat apples. Still, little pigs were different. After turnips, they liked apples best of all. "I'll tempt them with my description of the apples," he thought. And off he went to the pigs' house.

"Little pigs," he called out. "I've just had a fine big dinner! I'm not a hungry old wolf any more. I'm your friend. I can show you a place where the apples are easy to pick."

"Is that so?" said the first little pig, quite ready to believe in the wolf's change of heart.

"Is that so, indeed!" said his smart little brother. "Don't believe a word and keep

the chain on the door, if you please!"

"I'll meet you early tomorrow morning," continued the wolf, "and take you to the orchard. You've never seen such apples, all rosy red and sweet and crisp."

But the next day, the third little pig got up while the wolf was still asleep, nipped down to the orchard and filled his basket with lovely red apples. He was back home, long before the wolf had opened his eyes.

The wolf was so angry and so hungry by the afternoon that he decided on desperate measures. If he couldn't get into the little pigs' house through the door, he would enter by the chimney.

"Little pigs, little pigs," he called through the keyhole. "I'm off on my holidays. "Goodbye little pigs, goodbye!"

"Holidays, indeed!" snorted the third little pig. "We must be more than ever on our guard."

So that night the three little pigs sat listening in their kitchen, and presently they heard the wolf prowling round and round their little house.

"He's trying to get in," whispered the first little pig, and he trembled all over.

"He's climbing up on to the roof," whispered the second little pig, and the curl went out of his tail.

"I expect he has thought of the chimney," said the third little pig, and he spoke without any fear, for he was not only the smartest of the little pigs but also the bravest.

Then all three little pigs heard the scratching and scraping of the wolf's long, sharp claws on the roof.

"I knew it!" said the first little pig. "He is quite determined to get in!" And the curl went out of his tail too.

"Get out our big stew pan," was all the third little pig said.

And when this was done, he told his two frightened brothers to fill it with water and hang it on the hook over the fire.

Then the third little pig heaped more and more sticks on the fire so that the flames leaped up high, licking the big black pan. "Now, we're ready for him," said he.

When the second little pig began to understand what would happen to that bad old wolf if he did come down the chimney, the curl came back to his tail as he stared at the pot.

The wicked wolf landed in that stew pan with an enormous plop and splash! Then all three little pigs let down the big heavy lid.

The three little pigs gathered round the big black stew pan. All they could see of the bad wolf was his bushy tail.

"That's the end of him," said the first little pig.

"He won't trouble us again," said the second little pig.

"It's lucky for you that you have such a clever brother," said the third little pig.

And that really was the end of the wolf for one way or another he was never seen again.

Thumbelina

THERE WAS ONCE a young woman who had a nice little house of her own. She didn't want to share it with a husband, but she did long for a child to keep her company.

One day she heard about a wise old woman in the next village. "She is so wise and clever," her friend told her, "she's more like a witch but a very good one. Why don't you try her?"

So the young woman went to the good witch to ask for help.

"Cross my hand with silver," said the old dame, as soon as she was seated at the table, "and tell me what bothers you."

"I long for a little girl of my very own," said the young woman. "Is that too much to hope for?"

"It is not," said the witch. "Take this grain of barley-corn and plant it in a pot tonight. That's all you have to do."

"It's not much," said the young woman. "What shall I see in the morning?"

"You shall see what you shall see," said the wise old woman. "Now go!"

The young woman did exactly as she was told. Before she went to bed that night, she planted the barley-corn in a large blue pot and left it by the kitchen window. But she was so excited at the thought of what she might see in the morning that she scarcely slept a wink.

Very early the next day, she hurried into the kitchen. A tall tulip-like flower, with all its petals folded tight just as if it were still asleep, was growing out of her blue pot and, scarcely knowing why she did so, she bent down and kissed it.

No sooner had she done this than the petals began to unfold and there – oh there – in the centre of the flower sat a tiny girl-child. She was so tiny, no bigger than the woman's thumb, that she could sit quite comfortably and securely in the flower's heart.

The woman looked at her for a long time and then very gently took hold of her.

"Well," said she, "there is only one possible name for you. Thumbelina!"

Then she searched around for a suitable cradle for the tiny child and found, at last, a walnut-shell which she lined with pretty violet-leaves.

Now although Thumbelina was tiny, she was as bright as a cricket and the woman delighted in playing with her. She would set her on the table by the window and watch her as she amused herself by jumping from one daisy to another. At other times, Thumbelina would ask for a saucer filled with water so that she could play her favourite game of rowing. Laughing tenderly, the woman would place a broad leaf on the water and give her child two horse-hairs for oars so that Thumbelina could row from one side of the saucer to the other in her leaf-boat.

They were so happy together that the woman soon began to think of Thumbelina as her very own little girl.

Every night, she kissed her and put her back in her walnut-shell cradle, covering her up with a pretty yellow rose-leaf, which made a cosy eiderdown.

Now the woman's house was not far away from a stream where a family of ugly toads had their home. And one night Mother Toad came to the house and peered through the window of the very room where Thumbelina lay fast asleep in her cradle. How pretty she looked! Fat old Mother Toad couldn't take her eyes off her and all kinds of nonsense thoughts came into her ugly head. "My son would like her. She would make him a charming wife. Why not? It's time he found somebody to take care of him. Yes, yes, I said I would find him a suitable bride and now I have done just that!"

The big ugly Toad looked about her and saw that one of the window panes was broken. What a pity the woman had never thought to have it mended, but then it was summer-time and she had a feeling that fresh-air was good for her precious child.

So, there it was! Mother Toad had found a way to reach the little girl and soon she had hopped through the window and on to the table. It was no trouble at all to pick up the cradle and hop back through the window and into the garden. But not until she had left the garden and was safely home did she put down the cradle.

Home for Mother Toad and her son was the muddy bank of the stream and very unpleasant it was too – or would have been to anything but a toad.

"Croak, croak, cr–croak," said Mother Toad loudly. "Look, what I've brought you!" And her son, who was just as ugly but not nearly so big and strong, hopped over the mud to see what kind of insect his mother had brought him for supper.

"Croak!" said he, when he saw the tiny sleeping child. "Croak, croak," which meant that he would much rather she had been a fat, juicy fly.

"She'll make you a very pretty wife," said Mother Toad. "You are a lucky toad to have such a clever mother!"

Then the old Toad sat down to think of the wedding and to make plans for the reception. "You will be the envy of all other toads," she said to her son. "You should be grateful to your mother."

But her son was both lazy and stupid and he cared so little for his pretty bride-to-be that he began hopping away to search for insects.

"Croak, croak!" his mother said, in a disappointed way. "If you won't stay and take care of her I will have to take her out into the stream and put her on a water-lily leaf."

So Mother Toad carried the cradle into the water and swam with it to a broad leaf. Son Toad followed her because he was afraid of what she might do if he didn't.

"Rock the cradle," ordered Mother Toad. "Isn't she pretty? My, how soundly she sleeps!"

"Croak, brek-kek-kex!" said the young toad, which translated, meant, "I'm hungry and I want my supper."

The ugly toads left Thumbelina on the leaf, but then Mother Toad decided the cradle would be a nice bit of furniture for the bridal suite and turning back, she lifted Thumbelina out of it and laid her on the leaf.

As she swam away with the shell, she heard Thumbelina call out in fright. "She'll soon find out how lucky she is," she told herself. "It's not everyone who is fortunate enough to have her wedding arranged for her."

Poor Thumbelina! How bitterly she wept when she found herself all alone in the middle of the stream.

At last, her sobs attracted the attention of some little fishes. "You are to marry Mother Toad's fat lazy son," they told her. "We know all about it."

Thumbelina wept more than ever at this and the fishes, taking pity on her, nibbled the thick stalk that held the leaf anchored and set it free. Away went the leaf, spinning in the current and dancing over the rippling waves. It made a perfect boat and Thumbelina dried her eyes and began to enjoy herself.

On and on she sailed until a friendly
white butterfly fluttered down to speak to
her. It was so nice to have a companion
that Thumbelina tied her ribbon around
the butterfly. Now she had both a friend
and a sail.

But, oh dear, as the boat floated under
the branches of a tall tree, a horrid black
beetle-like creature swooped down and
made her his prisoner. The cockchafer, for
that was who he was, told her it was a case
of instant love. "Never," said he, as he
placed her on a leaf, "have I seen anything so pretty. I intend to marry you
right away."

Soon, his relatives came along to inspect Thumbelina. "Look at her waist!"
said his great-aunt. "What a skinny thing
it is. And she's only got four legs."

"I suppose you know what you are
doing!" said his grandfather. "But she's
quite the ugliest insect we've ever set
eyes on."

The young cockchafer took a second,
very close look at poor frightened Thumbelina. Had he made a mistake? Perhaps
he had. And without a word of apology,
he picked her up, and flew down to the
grass with her, leaving her on a daisy.

Thankfully, Thumbelina waited until
the ugly creature had gone back to his
relatives. "What a narrow escape that
was!" she told herself. "How I should have
hated being the wife of that shiny black
creature!" And she jumped down from the
daisy and began wandering through the
woods.

The shy delicate violets welcomed the
pretty child, and the bees showed her

where she could find honey. Overhead the birds sang to her of long summer days and blue skies and Thumbelina was suddenly happy.

"I shall stay here for ever," she told the flowers. "This is where I belong." The flowers nodded and smiled down on her but the bees warned her to beware of the winter. "Summer doesn't last," they told her. "Wait until winter comes. Winter is a terrible time in the woods. What will you do then?"

But Thumbelina refused to listen to them and so, when the cold winter wind came rushing through the woods, it took her by surprise.

"You should have listened to the bees," said the flowers, as they folded up their petals. "You should have listened."

Before the last of the birds flew away to seek the sunshine, he showed her how to weave a tiny house for herself. It wasn't much of a place for the roof was made of grass and the floor was a leaf. But it sheltered her from the cruel wind and it protected her from the snow.

How silent and lonely the woods were now! Thumbelina sat in her little shelter, shivering and frightened, as the big snow-flakes fell out of the grey sky.

"If I stay here I shall die of cold," she told herself at last. And she left her shelter and set off through the woods. Now, close to the woods was a large cornfield and here Thumbelina found herself at last. What a dreadful place it was with its great high stubble standing up out of the ground. How easy it was to get lost in such a forest!

Thumbelina began to wish she had never left her shelter but it was too late! She could not find her way out of such a deep forest and as she wandered this way and that, she suddenly came upon a small neat door in the ground. As she stood there, trembling with cold and ready to die of hunger, the door was suddenly opened by – who do you think – an elderly lady Fieldmouse.

"Gracious me!" said the old Fieldmouse. "Don't stand shivering there. Come inside."

Mistress Fieldmouse lived in great style in a hole which she had divided into a snug kitchen, larder and bedroom. And what is more, her larder was well stocked with golden corn.

"First, I'll give you something to eat," said she. And she brought out some of her corn. "Then you must tell me all about yourself."

Well, as soon as the old lady mouse had heard Thumbelina's sad story, she said, "You can stay with me. There's not much sweeping to do and as long as you tell me a fresh story each evening, you and I will get on very well."

So Thumbelina made her home with the kind-hearted old Fieldmouse and, by the end of the winter, had become quite fond of her.

As for the Fieldmouse, she looked upon pretty Thumbelina as her daughter and was determined to find her a suitable husband. "I know the very one for you," she declared, one evening. "And he's coming tomorrow to have a look at you. He's rich and handsome so do your best to please him for he will make you an excellent husband."

The next day the Fieldmouse went about in a flurry of high excitement.

"Who is he? What does he look like? Where does he live?" Thumbelina asked, as the old Fieldmouse set her down at the spinning wheel.

"His name is Mister Mole," said the Fieldmouse. "And he lives in his own house at the end of a long tunnel linked to my house. He has a very rich handsome appearance and is never at a loss for words. You'll like him, I'm sure."

But Thumbelina did not like Mister Mole. She was quite terrified by his large size, his sharp claws and his long quivering whiskers.

Mister Mole, for his part, thought Thumbelina would make him an excellent wife. It is true he could not see her very well, being extremely shortsighted, but that did not matter. She had a pretty, soft voice and would, he was sure, be very obedient.

"You must visit me tonight," he said, in his deep voice. "I'll be pleased to show you round your new home."

As Thumbelina followed the Fieldmouse along the dark tunnel, some hours later, she came upon a poor injured swallow. The Mole kicked him aside, but Thumbelina knelt beside the bird and whispered that she would take care of him if only he wouldn't die!

"I hate birds," said Mister Mole, as they reached his house. "I don't understand why they want to fly about in the sunshine. It is so much nicer under the ground. I never go out and you won't, either, once we are married."

Never to go out, never to see the green grass or the flowers again! How Thumbelina dreaded her wedding day! But although she was so unhappy, she did not forget the bird and, each night, when the old Fieldmouse was fast asleep, she brought

enough to leave the tunnel and fly away.

"I shall be gone before it is light," he said. "But I shall not forget you."

Thumbelina was kept at her weaving for the Fieldmouse was quite determined that she should go to Mister Mole with a splendid new wardrobe. "You are like a daughter to me," she would say. But the girl was now afraid of her and no longer sang as she went about her duties.

Mistress Fieldmouse kept a strict watch over her and it was not until the wedding day itself that Thumbelina dared to ask permission to go outside. "I should so much like to see the trees and the flowers for the last time," she added.

"Very well," said the Fieldmouse. "But don't stay long. There is still a great deal to do for the wedding feast."

So, for the last time, Thumbelina went into the fields and, as she gazed up at the sky, there was her old friend the swallow on his way south for the winter.

"Come with me, Thumbelina," he said, as he flew down to her. "A long journey lies ahead of us, but at the end of it is the beautiful Land of Flowers."

"I will come!" cried Thumbelina. "I am not afraid of anything except being married to rich Mister Mole." And she seated herself on the swallow's back.

The swallow soared into the sky. He flew over snow-clad mountains and across deep white valleys. He flew steadily and strongly for many hours until at last he came to the Land of Flowers.

"We are home," he told Thumbelina, as he glided gently to earth. "I told you it was beautiful."

Thumbelina saw how truly he had spoken. All about her were flowers – gentle, friendly flowers that nodded to her as if they had known her all their days.

him food and water.

Her tender care for the swallow brought its reward. One night, as she stroked his head, he told her that he was now strong

"Welcome to the Land of Flowers," said the handsome Elfin King of this wonderful place. And he swept off his golden crown and took her hand. "You are more lovely than any of my subjects."

Then, with great charm, he begged her to be his Queen.

"I will tell her story to the whole wide world," said the swallow, as he listened. "I will tell all the world how little Thumbelina found happiness."

"Do that," said the Elfin King. "And let it be known, too, that for a wedding present the King gave her a pair of silver wings so that she could fly with him from flower to flower."

The Nightingale

LONG, LONG AGO there was once a mighty Emperor. He ruled over a vast country called China, and he lived in a porcelain palace which was the most splendid in the whole world. The gardens of this magnificent palace were so huge that not even the fifty gardeners who tended them knew exactly where they ended.

Now beyond these gardens lay a great wood with tall trees that grew right down to the edge of the sea, and in one of these trees lived a nightingale. Whenever he sang in the evening the townsfolk, who had come to watch the ships anchored at sea, heard his song.

The sailors and the fishermen talked endlessly about the nightingale's song for, of course, they heard it most often. And scholars from other lands, who came to write about the mighty Emperor, his splendid porcelain palace and his wonderful gardens, wrote instead about the little grey nightingale in the woods.

One day a book fell into the Emperor's imperial hands. It began by praising the palace and the gardens but quite soon its author started writing about the nightingale. "No treasure," he wrote, "can compare with the nightingale's song."

The Emperor read these words twice over. Then he sent for his elder statesman.

"What's this?" exclaimed the Emperor. "What nightingale! I have never heard of it."

"Nor I," said the elder statesman.

"I command that he appear this very evening to sing before me," said the Emperor. "If not, the court will eat only boiled rice for a month."

Such a threat made the elder statesman tremble so he said very quickly, "Yes, Your Imperial Majesty. I understand."

And he bowed himself out of the throne room. But where was he going to find anyone who could tell him how to find this nightingale? He rushed as fast as his small feet and thin legs would take him up and down the corridors and into the huge banqueting halls in search of a courtier who might be able to help him.

But the courtiers were all too grand to walk in the woods and they knew nothing of the little grey bird.

The kitchens were the last place the elder statesman considered visiting for there only the most humble of the Emperor's servants worked. Finally, he put his head round the kitchen door, and began questioning the chief washer-up.

The washer-up nodded and called to his side a little kitchen-maid. Then he said, "Yes, my lord, I have heard of the nightingale from this young kitchen-maid. She knows the bird quite well."

"Can this be so!" exclaimed the old man happily. "Tell me, child, where we can find this wonderful singing bird and you shall be immediately promoted out of the kitchens into the corridors."

"He sings to me every night when I pass through the woods on my way to my mother's hut," replied the girl. "I know the tree where he perches."

"Today, little kitchen-maid, you are excused from all your duties," said the elder statesman grandly. "Prepare your-self to lead us to the nightingale."

So the little kitchen-maid wiped her hands on her ragged apron and led the elder statesman and a great number of the courtiers out of the palace and into the woods.

As they went along a cow began to low and one of the pages, who was accompanying his master, cried, "Listen! That's it! What a marvellous sound!"

But the little kitchen-maid said, "No, that is not the song of the nightingale. It is only a cow lowing to her calf."

Presently, some frogs, disturbed by the long procession, began croaking in the marshes and another of the pages cried, "Listen! Listen! I am the first to hear the nightingale's song!"

"All you hear is the croaking of frogs," said the kitchen-maid. "I will tell you when we come to the tree where the nightingale nests."

And so the procession moved on until, at last, the girl held up her hand. The elder statesman stopped so suddenly that the courtier behind him was bumped on the

head and there was some confusion before everybody was ready to look up into the tree.

"What a plain little grey bird!" whispered the fattest of the courtiers, who admired everything that was big and fat. But the elder statesman frowned at him severely, and the kitchen-maid called, "Nightingale, nightingale, will you come to the palace this evening and sing for our noble Emperor?"

"With very great pleasure," the nightingale answered.

The elder statesman sighed with relief when he heard this. Then he called up, "You will be given every honour. You *will* come?"

"I will come," answered the nightin-

gale, "although my song sounds best when heard in the woods."

"Never mind that!" whispered the fat courtier to his neighbour. "If he doesn't come we shall have to eat boiled rice for a month," and he shuddered.

After the meeting with the nightingale, the courtiers no longer stayed together but returned to the palace in pairs or small groups. Some walked slowly, quite charmed by the fresh green of the countryside. Others were so anxious to be back in the palace that they ran too fast and fell headfirst into ditches, or tore their fine robes on thorn bushes.

As for the elder statesman, he hurried as much as he could without losing dignity and so was more than a little breathless when, at last, he stood before his Emperor.

"The nightingale is coming, Your Imperial Majesty," he panted. "He will sing for you this very night."

So the Emperor ordered that a festival should be held in the bird's honour and the great hall be decorated with a thousand golden lamps and the most glorious of his flowers.

All this was done under the elder statesman's supervision, for he was responsible to the Emperor for everything that went right or wrong inside the imperial palace.

As darkness fell, the Emperor entered the great hall and seated himself on his golden throne. Then all the courtiers took their places and all the ladies-in-waiting and those of the page boys who could squeeze themselves in. Then the elder statesman opened all the windows and set up the nightingale's golden perch. Everybody waited in silence until, suddenly, a little grey bird flew in through the window.

Without fuss or bother, the nightingale went to the golden perch and began to sing. Words cannot truthfully describe the beauty of the grey bird's song. But it can be said that all the naughtiest and most restless of the boy pages sat as if they had been changed into statues. Some of the ladies-in-waiting were so overcome that they brought out their smelling salts.

As for the Emperor, he was enchanted and so moved that tears came to his eyes. "You may ask for anything," he told the nightingale, at the end of the song. "Anything at all and it shall be yours."

"The tears I have seen in Your Imperial Majesty's eyes are reward enough," replied the nightingale.

But this did not satisfy the Emperor. "Hang my golden slippers about his neck," he ordered the elder statesman.

"No," said the nightingale. "I have no use for such a valuable gift." And he began to sing again.

At the end of the nightingale's second song, the Emperor was more than ever determined to reward the bird. "My whole palace is yours," he said. "You shall have a golden cage of your own and sing to me each night."

"The fresh green woods are my true home," said the nightingale.

"That may be so," replied the Emperor, "and you will be at liberty to go there twice in one day, but at night you must return."

Now everybody knew that whatever the Emperor desired would come to pass; even the little grey bird of the woods knew this. So he submitted to being placed in a golden cage. Even when he was allowed to fly away into the woods he was not truly at liberty for golden threads were fastened to his legs. The threads were held by twelve servants whose lives depended on holding them very tightly.

The nightingale was now famous throughout the entire empire. At street corners, poets read aloud their verses about him and countless proud parents gave their first born children the name "Nightingale".

The Emperor himself encouraged his court to give the plain grey bird every honour and would, on no account, retire to his sleeping chamber until the nightingale had sung to him.

So many books arrived at the palace about the nightingale that the Emperor set aside a special room in his palace for them and this was always known as "The Nightingale's Library".

One day, a package arrived for the Emperor which he thought at once must be yet another book. It was not a book, however, but a box in which sat a mechanical nightingale whose head and body were studied with precious stones.

"Very pretty," said the Emperor. Then he looked at it more closely and saw that round the bird's neck was a ribbon on which the following words, in tiny letters, were inscribed:
The Emperor of Japan sends you his wonderful singing bird to which no other can compare.

Now the Emperor was annoyed and upset when he read these words for he had no liking for the Japanese Emperor. "We'll see about that," he said. And calling for his watchmaker, he ordered him to wind up the glittering bird with the golden key which was also in the box.

No sooner was this done than the brilliant artificial bird began to sing and as it did so, its glittering diamond and ruby tail moved up and down.

"Beautiful, quite beautiful!" exclaimed the watchmaker. And indeed the mechanical bird's song was charming.

"Hmmm!" said the Emperor. "Let me hear it just once more."

So once again the bird sang and every note was perfect and very tuneful. Some of the courtiers heard the mechanical bird's song. "It sings just as beautifully as the real bird," they declared, "and is much more attractive. Look at these diamonds and sapphires and gorgeous rubies!"

That night, when the little nightingale of the woods came to sing to his Emperor, the Emperor said that he must sing a duet with the brilliant mechanical bird.

The real nightingale did his best but

as he never sang the same song twice, his efforts to match the notes coming from the bejewelled bird were a dismal failure.

For the first time the Emperor looked with disfavour on his woodland bird and turned away from him.

As the weeks went by, the true nightingale was rarely summond into the imperial presence. In fact, he fell so completely out of favour that when at last he stayed in the woods all day and all night he wasn't even missed. His escape was made possible, of course, through the carelessness of the twelve servants, who no longer troubled to hold on to the twelve golden strings fastened to his legs.

No one was bothered when the real nightingale disappeared. Now that their Emperor had the beautiful shining mechanical bird, which sang to order, there was nothing to fear. As long as the Emperor was happy, the court was happy. And if the court was happy, the people in the towns and cities were happy.

And the Emperor *was* happy; he had the artificial bird, whose song matched the real nightingale's song in beauty, and he could hear it whenever he wished.

The mechanical bird sat on a golden cushion on a table at his side and the watchmaker, who had been given the rank of "Imperial Nightingale Winder", was always at hand to turn the golden key.

The Emperor was so delighted with his new toy that he held another festival, but this time he invited all the people from the city. So many came that they filled the tulip garden. The Emperor looked down on them from his balcony and showed them the brilliant bird. Then the Imperial Nightingale Winder used the golden key to wind up the bird and it began its song for the hundred and twenty second time.

Of course all the people were enchanted – except perhaps the fishermen who were accustomed to the real nightingale's song, and the kitchen-maid, now promoted to polisher-in-chief of the corridors, who still went into the woods to visit her old mother, and often spoke to the grey bird.

Poets read their verses about the artificial nightingale at the street corners and everybody talked and praised it. Those who could afford it sent the bird magnificent presents, which pleased the Emperor.

Then something really dreadful happened. One evening, the watchmaker wound up the shining nightingale just as usual. Instead of a beautiful song, there came only a loud ugly whir-r-r, which set the Emperor's teeth on edge.

The watchmaker stared at the bird in dismay. "I'm sorry, Your Majesty," he said, "but the works have worn out; the tiny wheels whirr round and round, it is true, but they have lost the power to make music."

"Nonsense, I won't have it!" exclaimed the Emperor, and he looked so angry and so threatening that the watchmaker turned pale.

"All is not lost," he said hastily. "It is possible that I can do some repairs."

"You had better!" said the Emperor.

"You had better!" said the elder statesman, who liked to repeat his Emperor's words. "See to it right away."

The watchmaker carried the bird to his workshop and with great skill and patience pulled it to pieces and then put it together again. All this took a long time. The Emperor grew more and more miserable without his bird and so too did the court who feared they would soon be eating nothing but boiled rice.

At last the watchmaker was ready to face his lord and master. "The bird will sing," he said proudly, "but do not, I beg you, have me wind it up more than once a year."

This state of affairs went on for five years or more. Every care was taken to preserve the life of the mechanical bird and it continued to sing most beautifully, but only on the Emperor's official birthdays.

Now the Emperor was growing quite old and one day he fell ill. As he lay there in his splendid bed with the long red velvet curtains closed, he began to think of the real little nightingale. "How lovely his song, was," he told himself. "Oh, if only I could hear it again I believe I could cheat Death and be strong again."

Then he called out for music – for the song of his nightingale. The watchmaker came running with the mechanical bird and placed it on a silken cushion beside the Emperor.

"Let it sing for me," whispered the Emperor. "I know it is but a month since my official birthday but I must hear its song."

The Imperial Nightingale Winder wound up the glittering gorgeous bird; its tail moved up and down; it began to sing, then there was a whir-r-r and a cr-crack and the song was over. So too was the life of the artificial nightingale.

Death was now very close to the mighty Emperor. A ghostly spectre, he sat upon the Emperor's bed and he put the Emperor's golden crown on his own head. Then he took the Emperor's golden sword and held it between long wraith-like fingers.

"Sing to me!" gasped the Emperor. "Sing me your beautiful song, little nightingale."

All at once the lovely song of the real nightingale filled the room. He sat on the branch of a cherry tree just outside the window and he sang of all the most wonderful things in nature, of the green trees and the wild flowers and the blue sky.

The Emperor raised his head, and Death took off the golden crown and put down the golden sword. He would come again for the old man but not now – not perhaps for many years.

On and on sang the nightingale, and Death floated away up the chimney and the Emperor sat up in his gorgeous bed and held out his arms to the little grey bird.

"Thank you! thank you!" he said. "I

treated you so badly and yet you have come to me when I most needed you."

"You wept once at the beauty of my song," said the nightingale. "That was something I could never forget."

Then the nightingale began to sing once more and the Emperor sank back on his silken pillows and fell into a deep, peaceful sleep.

All through the night the elder statesman and the courtiers waited outside the royal bedchamber in fear and trembling.

"He must be dead," they whispered to each other. "Who will enter first?"

"I will," said the elder statesman. And he went in, expecting to find his Emperor quite dead. But there he was – sitting up in bed and smiling.

"Good morning," said he. "What a lovely day!"

So the mighty Emperor was restored to life by the song of the nightingale of the woods who, from then on, came to him each night. The mechanical bird was soon forgotten – except perhaps by the watchmaker, who secretly mourned that he was no longer Imperial Nightingale Winder.

Goldilocks and the Three Bears

NCE UPON A TIME there was a little girl who liked finding out things for herself. She had bright golden curls and everybody called her Goldilocks.

One day Goldilocks went for a walk in the woods. "I'll go down this path and find out where it leads," she said to herself.

Well, it led her straight to the prettiest little cottage she had ever seen.

"Oh!" said Goldilocks, and she said it very loudly. "Oh! What a pretty little house! I must find out who lives there." And in she went – without knocking!

Now this pretty little house belonged to a family of Bears, Father Bear, Mother Bear and Baby Bear. They had all gone for a walk before breakfast. But Mother Bear had put the porridge in three bowls to let it get cold, which is the way Bears like to eat porridge.

Goldilocks saw the porridge and she saw that there were three chairs in the cosy room. "I'll think I'll sit down," she said to herself.

First, she tried the very big chair. But, oh dear me, that was far too big. Then she tried the middle-sized chair and that was much too hard. At last she sat down in the very small chair and – crash! The legs came off and she tumbled on to the floor.

Naughty little Goldilocks didn't even try to put the chair together again. Instead she went over to the table and sniffed the porridge.

"My!" she thought to herself, "I'm so hungry. And that porridge does smell ever so good!"

So she picked up the biggest spoon and dipped it into the biggest bowl. But, oh dear, the porridge in that big, big bowl was much too hot. Then she picked up the middle-sized spoon and dipped it into the middle-sized bowl. But, oh dear, that was much too salty. Finally, she picked up the weeny-teeny spoon and dipped it into the weeny-teeny bowl – and the porridge tasted exactly right.

With a sigh of contentment, greedy Goldilocks gobbled up every bit of the porridge in the weeny-teeny bowl.

After so much to eat, Goldilocks began to feel very sleepy. She yawned and then went off upstairs to find somewhere to rest.

Now the Three Bears had their bedroom upstairs. There were three beds in the room, all different sizes.

First, Goldilocks tried the very big, huge bed, but, oh dear, that was really far too big.

Then she tried the middle-sized bed, but, oh dear, that was far too lumpy. At last, she flung herself down on the weeny-teeny bed – and that was exactly her size. It felt so comfortable that she shut her eyes and was soon fast asleep.

Now, as Goldilocks slept, who should come home from their walk but the Three Bears.

"Somebody's been sitting on my chair," growled Father Bear, in his deep voice.

"Somebody's been sitting in my chair," said Mother Bear, in her soft gentle voice.

"And somebody's been sitting on my chair and broken it all up!" cried Baby Bear, in his squeaky voice. And he began to sob.

Then the Three Bears went over to the table and stared down at their porridge bowls.

"Somebody's been tasting my porridge," growled Father Bear, in his deep voice.

"Somebody's been tasting my porridge," said Mother Bear, in her gentle voice.

"And somebody's been at my porridge and eaten it all up," cried Baby Bear, in his squeaky voice.

The Three Bears began to wonder what they would find upstairs in the bedroom.

"Somebody has been lying on my bed," growled Father Bear, "and look! The pillow is on the floor."

"Somebody," said Mother Bear, in her gentle voice, "has been lying on my bed. Just look at these crumpled sheets!"

Then all three Bears went over to the weeny-teeny bed which belonged to Baby Bear.

"Somebody *is* lying on my bed," squeaked Baby Bear. "Look! Look!"

Big growly Father Bear, gentle, middle-sized Mother Bear and weeny-teeny Baby Bear stared down at the sleeping little girl.

Suddenly, Goldilocks opened her eyes. Then she sat up. Then she jumped out of bed and ran away down the stairs as fast as she could go.

Away she ran through the woods as if a hundred bears were chasing her. And, do you know, she never stopped running until she was safely home.

You may be sure that was the very last time Goldilocks walked in the woods or went into a strange house without first being invited. You see, she was afraid she might meet the Three Bears again!

The Little Matchgirl

THE STORYTELLER had been telling his wonderful stories all afternoon, "One more," he said finally, as the children begged him to go on. "Just one about a little girl whose love for her grandmother was the only beautiful thing in her life. Then her grandmother died and went to heaven and the little girl had no one in the world to love.

"She lived under a roof that was stuffed with rags and straw to keep out the wind and rain and she had a father who beat her for no reason at all.

"One day, it was the last day of the Old Year, her father sent her out to sell bundles of matches. Almost certainly, she started out wearing old slippers. Perhaps, who knows, they had once belonged to her dead grandmother, for they were so big for her that she soon lost them in the deep snow. How bitterly cold it was that day! How quickly the people hurried past – without even seeing her! Soon there was nobody in the street and the little Match-girl, half frozen with cold and weak with hunger, leant up against a post, her fingers almost too numb to hold the bundle of matches. Never before had she dared to strike one of her own matches, but now she took one out of the bundle and struck it. How it spluttered and burned! It was like a fire, a real fire that warmed her icy fingers. But then the little flame went

out. Quickly, the Matchgirl took another of her matches.

"What a marvellous sight she saw in its bright flame! A whole roasted goose set on a dish and ready to be served swam before her eyes. But then, as she took up her knife and fork, the match went out.

"Trembling, she lit her third match and there was a Christmas tree, with hundreds of candles, shining like the heavenly stars. And she began thinking of her good, kind grandmother in heaven.

"Everything was forgotten now but the need to light yet another match. And there, oh there, in its wonderful bright flame was her very own grandmother. Fearful of losing her, the Matchgirl lit

every one of her matches, smiling happily as her grandmother took her in her loving arms. . . ."

The storyteller paused – for now it was nearly, but not quite, the very end of his story.

"Was – was she still smiling?" asked one of the boys, "when they found her, all frozen dead in the snow?"

"Yes," said the storyteller. "On her face was the most beautiful, heavenly smile!"

Snow-White and the Seven Dwarfs

 QUEEN SAT BY HER open window. It was winter and the snow-flakes fell like soft feathers on the ledge. As she sewed, she pricked her finger and a single drop of blood fell upon the snow. "I wish, oh, how I wish that I might be blessed with a child," she thought. "A little girl who would have skin as white as this snow, with lips as red as my blood and hair as black as this window-frame. How happy I would be!"

In time, the Queen's fondest wish was granted, and the baby was so pretty, all pink and white with hair as black as ebony, that the Queen named her Snow-White.

The King shared his wife's joy in their little daughter and they were a happy, united family until, one sad day, the Queen fell ill and died. Shortly afterwards, the King brought home a new wife to grace his palace.

"How beautiful she is!" the servants whispered to each other. "But she is not like the old Queen. She has strange powers, that one!"

In fact, the handsome woman who now ruled over the palace was a witch with a nature so cruel and envious that soon she became greatly feared.

Now among some of the strange objects she brought with her to the palace was a truly wonderful magic mirror. No one dared look into this mirror except, of course, the Queen herself. It hung on the wall of a lonely turret room which she alone used.

Every morning the Queen went up to her secret room in the palace and questioned the mirror, saying,

"*Mirror, mirror on the wall,*
Who is the fairest of us all?"

And the magic mirror would reply,
"*Thou art the fairest of them all.*"

Secure in the knowledge that her mirror would not lie to her, the proud Queen chose to ignore Snow-White, who was growing more and more lovely with the passing years.

Imagine her jealous anger when, upon questioning her mirror one morning, it told her,

"*My Lady Queen, thou still art fair,*
But none to Snow-White can compare."

"Snow-White!" she spat out the name as she paced up and down like a caged tigress. "Snow-White! So long as she lives I can only be second best!"

Then controlling her rage, she went to the stables to look for one of her huntsmen.

"You must take my stepdaughter into the forest," she told the horrified man. "Ride out with her today, kill her, and bring me her heart so that I may know the deed is well and truly done."

The huntsman was much too afraid of the spiteful Queen to argue. Saddling Snow-White's pony, he called the girl and told her they were going riding.

Mounted on her favourite pony, Snow-White followed the huntsman into the deepest part of the forest. When he told her to dismount, she asked, "Why here? It is so dark with all these tall trees blotting out the sun."

"The Queen has ordered me to kill you," said the huntsman, drawing his long knife. "It grieves me to put an end to such a young life, but she gives me no choice."

Now, despite his words, the huntsman could not remain deaf to Snow-White's tearful cry for mercy. And muttering an oath, he suddenly dropped his knife. "Go then," he said, "but do not attempt to return to the palace or else we shall both lose our heads."

All day, Snow-White wandered through the forest until, as darkness fell, she stumbled upon a little house. The door swung open, but no one answered her timid knock and, finally, she went inside.

How neat and tidy it was! In one room, seven small chairs were arranged around a polished table, and seven pairs of slippers lay side by side on the hearth. In another, seven small white beds stood in a neat row from wall to window, and, at the sight of them, Snow-White gave a weary sigh and dropped down on the nearest. Soon she was fast asleep.

She awoke to find seven little men

staring down at her. But their faces were kind and friendly and Snow-White sat up, not in the least afraid, and quickly told them her story. The seven dwarfs, for that was who they were, listened quietly. At the end of it, they said, "You are welcome to stay with us. Make this your home – only give us your promise that you will darn our socks and have supper ready for us on our return from the mines each night."

"I promise!" cried Snow-White, clapping her hands. "I will take good care of you." And the seven dwarfs said, "And we will take good care of you."

But what of the evil Queen? As she stood by her window, the huntsman came to her. "The deed is done," he said, and he showed her the heart of a wild beast which he had killed on his homeward journey through the forest.

Smiling, the Queen gazed out over the royal gardens. She was now the fairest of all women in the land. But that, alas, was not what the mirror told her the next morning.

"In the forest where seven dwarfs dwell
Snow-White is alive and well.
Thou art fair, oh Lady Queen
But she's the fairest ever seen,"
said the mirror.

Black and purple with rage, the Queen turned away from the mirror and sat down to think how she might destroy Snow-White. By means of her witchcraft, she changed herself into a brown-faced gypsy woman and taking a tray, filled it with pretty laces. Then she went to the house of the seven dwarfs.

"Buy my pretty laces!" she called out in wheedling tones, and Snow-White opened the door immediately, her eyes shining at the sight of the brightly coloured laces.

"I'll take the red ones," she said. And the gypsy woman laced them about her, pulling them so tightly that Snow-White could scarcely breathe, and so fell senseless to the ground.

When the dwarfs returned from the mines, they found her, lying on the ground as if dead.

"Cut the laces!" cried one dwarf.

"Pour water on her face," cried another. And when this was done Snow-White came back to life.

"We were only just in time," the little men told her. "You must never open the door while we are away. That was the evil Queen's doing, and no doubt she will come again to destroy you."

Poor Snow-White! How could she possibly guess that the friendly, stout countrywoman, who came calling the very next day, was none other than the Queen in disguise?

But she did not run to the door at once to open it. "What do you want?" she called through the window. "My little dwarfs have forbidden me to open the door."

"I have something to show you," replied the old woman, and from under her shawl she brought out the prettiest pink comb Snow-White had ever seen. It was decorated with tiny coloured stones that sparkled and glittered in the bright sunshine. The girl couldn't take her eyes off the comb.

"Oh, it is lovely!" she exclaimed.

"Come outside and let me try it in your dark hair," said the woman. "Your little dwarfs won't grudge you such a pretty trifle."

"No, of course not!" Snow-White cried. And closing the window she ran to the door and opened it.

Now the comb was indeed very pretty but it was a poisonous comb which the Queen had conjured up by means of witchcraft. No sooner did she fix it in the girl's hair than the poison began to spread throughout her body, and she collapsed on the ground. With an evil laugh, the Queen then vanished into the forest.

That day the dwarfs left off their digging earlier than usual and so it was not very long afterwards that they tramped homewards. When they found Snow-White on the ground, they guessed at once that the wicked Queen had paid her a visit.

"Take out the comb!" cried one dwarf.

"Give her salt water to drink," cried another. And so quickly did they act that the poison was overcome and Snow-White was saved.

The dwarfs lectured and spoilt Snow-White in turns. Then the eldest said, "When the Queen looks in that magic mirror of hers, she will learn that you are still alive. Then she will come again to our cottage."

"This time I promise not to open the door," Snow-White declared.

The dwarfs were right. The jealous Queen did try again and this time she made certain that Snow-White would die. Alone in her secret room, she studied her black book of spells and recipes until she found one which made her smile triumphantly.

"That's it!" she gloated. "An apple so round and rosy that no one can resist it – a poisonous apple, one bite of which is fatal! Now, I have her!"

When the apple was ready, the Queen changed herself into a fat old farmer's wife, filled a basket with apples and placed the round rosy red apple on top. Then she

went to the dwarfs' house in the forest.

"I cannot come out," Snow-White told her, as soon as she saw the smiling grey-haired old woman. And she leant out of the window and gazed longingly at the apples.

"Try one!" said the woman. And she took a bite out of the magic apple, as if to prove it was harmless. Then she tossed it to Snow-White.

Snow-White bit into the apple and almost at once collapsed on to the floor.

Satisfied that nothing could save her, the Queen gave an evil chuckle and disappeared into the forest.

When the dwarfs found Snow-White, she was already dead, and they wept and wrung their hands. "How beautiful she is, even in death!" they whispered. And that night they kept watch around her still body. In the flickering light of their candles, Snow-White seemed to them so lovely that they could not bear to think of her buried in the cold dark earth.

"Let us make a glass coffin for her," said one of the dwarfs at last. "She is as beautiful now as she was when she took care of us."

"Then we can look upon her each day," said another of the dwarfs.

So the seven dwarfs made a glass case for Snow-White and before placing her gently inside, they inscribed on it the words, *Here lies a King's Daughter*, in letters of gold, so that all who saw it would honour a Princess.

No longer did they set out each day, with pick and shovel, for the mines. Instead they mounted guard over the glass case and so sad were they that scarcely a word passed between them.

Now, one day, as the seven dwarfs stood round the coffin, stiff and straight, like sentries on duty, a Prince came riding through the forest. Greatly astonished at the strange sight of seven little men guarding a glass coffin, the Prince dismounted so that he might find out more about the extraordinary spectacle.

"Who is she?" he asked, gazing down on Snow-White. "How beautiful she is! Can she really be dead?"

"She is a king's daughter," the dwarfs told him. "Her name is Snow-White and we love her and will spend the rest of our days doing her honour."

Never, in all his life, had the young Prince seen such a beautiful girl and as he looked at her a great longing swept over him.

"Let me take her back to my palace," he said to the dwarfs. "Her beauty should not be hidden away. Her story will become a legend among my people."

But the dwarfs could not bear the thought of losing Snow-White.

"You are a Prince," they said, "and no doubt rich and powerful. We are only humble little men. But we know how to love. Snow-White must stay with us. She belongs here in the forest."

The Prince rode sadly away when he saw that the dwarfs were determined to keep Snow-White. He could not, however, forget her and, the next day, he returned with his attendants.

The kind-hearted dwarfs were upset by his pale face and sad eyes as he spoke to them. "I cannot live without your Snow-White," he told them. "Have pity on me! Allow my servants to carry her back to my palace."

At this, the dwarfs withdrew some distance to talk among themselves.

"Perhaps we have been too selfish," said one.

"The young man must love her almost as much as we do," said another.

And, finally, they agreed among themselves that the Prince should take Snow-White back to his own country. But as his servants raised the coffin to their shoulders, one of them stumbled and the Prince cried out in anger, "Take care! Take care!"

And then, oh then, something strange and wonderful happened. The lovely girl in the glass case opened her eyes! She was breathing again! She was alive! The poisonous piece of apple had fallen out of her mouth as the coffin tilted.

How the forest rang with the cheers of the seven dwarfs as they helped her to sit up.

"I have been asleep so long," she said, hugging each of the dwarfs in turn. Then, glancing shyly at the handsome young Prince, she asked who he was.

"He loved you so well," the dwarfs told her, "that he vowed he could not live without you."

"I loved you in death," declared the Prince, stepping forward. "And now I love you a thousand times more in life!"

Snow-White turned to her little men, and they said, "Go with him, dear Snow-White, he will take care of you far better than we can."

So the Prince and Snow-White were married, soon after, in great splendour, and when the evil Queen heard of the wedding by means of her magic mirror, she fell into such a rage that she began smouldering away until all that remained was a heap of grey ashes.

The Four Musicians

HERE WAS ONCE a donkey who had worked hard all his life to please his master. When he grew too old to move smartly, his master took to beating him and, at last, the old donkey made up his mind to run away.

Now, on the next farm, there was an old hunting dog and he, too, had served his master faithfully, But when he grew too fat to keep up with the other hounds in the pack, his master told him he was going to be retired. Unable to face the disgrace, he decided to run away.

Donkey and Dog met on the road that led to a big town.

"My master took to beating me for nothing," said Donkey, as they fell into conversation, "so I'm running away."

"I'm running away, too," said Dog. "My master was going to retire me."

"Let's team up together," suggested Donkey. "I'm on my way to town to start up a band. The gift for music runs in our family, you know." And he brayed loudly.

"My bark is so loud and musical that it attracts people from miles around. I'll be a worthy member of your band," said Dog.

The two new friends went on down the road, side by side, until they came upon a sadly bedraggled little cat. Her fur was

wet and her eyes half-shut.

"What a sight!" said Donkey. "You look half-drowned."

"I was," said Cat, "in a pail of water and by the very woman at whose feet I've laid a thousand mice or more."

"I suppose your output fell off!" said Dog sympathetically.

"I'm not as quick as I used to be," admitted Cat.

"Why don't you join us," said Donkey. "We're going to form a band."

"I'd like to," said Cat, and she purred softly.

After a few miles, they were hailed by a handsome Cock, perched on a garden fence.

"Cock-a-doodle-doo! Where are you three going?" he enquired.

"We're off to the big town," said Donkey, "to form a band."

"I'll join you," said Cock, "for I've just learnt that I'm going to be their Sunday dinner." And he flew down onto Donkey's broad back. "And all because I gave up being their alarm clock!" he added bitterly. "My crowing isn't quite so alarming these days."

"You'll be a splendid member of the band I mean to form," said Donkey.

As it grew dark, the four friends came to a deep forest and Donkey suggested that they camp under the trees for the night.

"I'll keep watch," said Cock. And, as the friends settled under a tree, he flew up to a high branch.

"I can see a house," he called down to them, after a few minutes, "with a light in the window."

"It would be very pleasant to sleep under a proper roof," said Cat.

"Let's go and see who lives there," said Dog. "We can look through the

window first before going round to the door."

Now the house in the forest was the headquarters of some fierce robbers. They were so wild and desperate that nobody had the courage to try and capture them. They came and went, as free as the wind, drinking and feasting whenever they were at home.

The four friends approached the house with caution and when they came to the window, Cat jumped on Donkey's back so that she could see into the room. Then they retreated to a distance and she made her report.

"I saw four men," she said, "terrible villains they looked, with knives and pistols lying on the table as they ate. They would kill us, I'm sure, if they knew we were here." And she hissed nervously.

"They're robbers, no doubt of it," said Dog, and he bared his yellow teeth.

"In that case," said Donkey, "we must make a plan. I suggest we wait until their light goes out. Then we launch our attack as they sleep."

And somewhat doubtfully, Cat and Cock agreed.

"Don't forget," said Dog, "I can bite. And you, Cat, can scratch, and you, Cock, can peck and peck. So keep up your courage!"

As soon as the light in the window went out, the four friends advanced on the house. Donkey used his powerful hind legs to kick in the window and, as the drunk and sleepy robbers reached for their knives, Cat spat and scratched their hands,

while Cock pecked their heads and Dog bit their legs. As for Donkey, he brayed and kicked out wildly.

The noise and confusion in that dark room was something to remember! Certain that they were being attacked by demons, the robbers took to their heels, tumbling over each other, as they made a dash for the forest.

When they had the place to themselves, the four friends sat down at the table and enjoyed the remnants of the robbers' feast. Then they went to bed.

In the morning, they looked over the house. Donkey found an old piano and Dog found a set of drums and a violin with broken strings.

"What do you say?" said Donkey, as they sat down to breakfast. "Shall we stay here and form our band?"

"We agree," said Cock and Cat.

And after breakfast, Donkey called his musicians together and soon they were practising hard.

So that's how it was and if, by chance, you hear the sound of music in a certain forest, you can be sure it's our four musicians having a wonderful time.

127

Aladdin and his Wonderful Lamp

A LONG TIME AGO, in one of China's big cities, there lived a boy called Aladdin. His father had been a tailor, and Aladdin might have learnt the trade if only he had put his mind to it. But he was a wild, thoughtless boy, too fond of playing in the streets to worry about trying to earn his living.

After his father died, his mother took in sewing and though she worked hard from morning to night she made so little money that they were always poor.

One day, as Aladdin gossiped with one of his friends, a tall bearded stranger, wearing a turban, stopped to watch him.

The next day the stranger appeared again in the narrow street where Aladdin most often played and this time he spoke to the boy. "Is your father called Mustapha?" he enquired. "And is he not a tailor?"

"That was my father's name," Aladdin said. "But he died some time ago – and, yes, he was a tailor."

"Alas," cried the stranger, throwing his arms around Aladdin. "Mustapha was my brother. I have been searching all over the world for him and now you tell me he is dead!"

"You must meet my mother," Aladdin cried, greatly excited at the thought of having an uncle. "We live quite close."

The stranger nodded and taking out some money pressed it into Aladdin's hand. "I will come tonight," he said. "I am rich and I would like to help you."

Now the tall bearded stranger was really a magician. He had come to the city to search for a suitable boy whom he could safely trust to carry out his orders. It seemed to him that Aladdin was just the very boy.

That night he arrived at Aladdin's house with gifts for the widow and two gold pieces for Aladdin.

The widow was so overcome by the generous gifts that she asked very few questions. "I did not know my poor dead husband had a brother," was all she said. "And we are fortunate indeed that you have found us."

"I hope my nephew is a good, hard-working boy," said the magician.

Aladdin hung his head in shame as his mother began to weep. "He is good for nothing," she sobbed. "Although he is old enough to do a man's work, he spends all his time in the street."

"Then I must try to help him," said the false uncle. "Perhaps I can find him a shop. I am sure a shop would not be too difficult for him to look after."

"I'd like that," said Aladdin. "I'd like a shop of my own very much indeed!"

It was then agreed that the next morning Aladdin should take his uncle around the city. Not only would it be a chance to show him the sights but they could, at the same time, see if there were any suitable

shops to be purchased.

The next morning, Aladdin was up and about much earlier than usual. He kept watch at the door until he saw his uncle's tall figure in the distance. Then he ran to greet him.

"What would you like to see first?" Aladdin asked. "There are some beautiful palaces and gardens in this city."

After walking through a number of gardens and down long narrow cobbled streets, Aladdin began to think about his new shop. He was disappointed that so far his uncle had not mentioned it.

"What about the shop?" he asked, at last. "We have not yet talked about it. Shall we go into the busy streets around the Sultan's palace? Shall we, uncle?"

"Not yet, nephew," replied the magician. "You have shown me many wonderful sights. Now I would like to be your guide. There is a place outside the city walls which I have long wished to visit."

Then the magician took a firm grasp of Aladdin's arm and led him out of the city. They walked some distance until they came at last to a lonely, desolate place.

"I have never been so far out of the city

before," Aladdin said, feeling suddenly afraid. "What kind of a place is this, uncle? Why have you brought me here?"

The narrow valley in which they now found themselves was hemmed in by tall threatening black mountains and Aladdin could not stop himself from shivering. He became even more afraid when his uncle pointed to some stone steps and urged him forward. "Come," said he, "there is nothing to be afraid of. I have watched you at play and I know you're a boy with plenty of courage."

When they reached the bottom of the steps, the magician caught hold of Aladdin's arm. "I am about to show you marvels that will astonish you!" he exclaimed.

Then he told Aladdin to gather some dry sticks so that he might make a fire. Aladdin obeyed, and when there was a great heap of them, the magician bent down and lit them.

As soon as the fire was blazing merrily, the magician threw some greenish powder on the flames and at the same time murmured strange words which made no sense at all to the watching boy.

Almost at once, however, they were engulfed in thick smoke and the ground under their feet began to shake. Aladdin stood, petrified with fear, unable to move. He shut his eyes, thinking his last moment had come. When he opened them, he saw that between himself and his uncle was a square, flat stone, with a big brass ring fixed in the centre of it.

Aladdin stared down at the broad stone. "Uncle! Uncle!" he exclaimed. "What has happened? That – stone! Why have you brought me here?"

"Lift the stone by the brass ring," ordered the magician, in a voice so harsh that Aladdin shrank away from him. "But listen first to what I have to say. Beneath this stone lies a deep well. When you reach the bottom, you will see a door. Pass through the door and into a great cave. Do not touch the walls of this cave or you will die. Beyond the cave lies a wonderful garden and there you may help yourself to the jewelled fruits that hang from the trees."

"Do you promise that no harm will come to me?" Aladdin burst out.

"Wait," commanded his uncle. "You have not yet heard what you must do for me. You must pass through this garden into another, smaller cave and there you will find a lamp which burns in a niche of the wall. It is this lamp which you must bring me. I want nothing but the lamp."

"I understand," said Aladdin.

"Then take hold of the brass ring," said the magician, in a softer voice. "And at the same time repeat aloud the names of your father and your grandfather."

Aladdin obeyed, trembling with excitement. To his surprise, the heavy stone was easy to lift and just as he was about to climb down into the well, his uncle took a ring from his finger and bade Aladdin wear it. "It will protect you," he said, "from all harm."

Boldly, Aladdin went into the deep well, climbing downwards by means of narrow stone steps hewn out of the rock.

He found the door at the bottom of the steps and passing through this was soon crossing a vast cave. Without touching anything, he passed from this great cave into a wondrous garden, so brilliantly lit that Aladdin gasped, blinking in the dazzling light that came from hundreds of coloured fruits suspended from the branches of trees.

But the fruits were not for eating. They were fashioned out of precious stones and, with a shout of joy, Aladdin began filling his pockets. His uncle had spoken truly. Here was a fortune just for the plucking!

When, at last, he remembered the lamp, he left the wonderful garden and presently found himself in a small dark cave where, in a niche, stood an old lamp. Its light was so feeble compared to the brilliance of the glowing fruits that Aladdin could scarcely believe his uncle wanted such a worthless looking object.

"I'd best do as he asks," he told himself, and taking down the lamp from its stand, he put out the light and carried it, with his other treasures, to the bottom of the well.

Up the steep narrow steps he climbed until he glimpsed his uncle waiting for him at the entrance.

"The lamp! The lamp!" cried the magician. "Hand me up the lamp."

"No – not until you have pulled me out of this well," Aladdin shouted back.

When the magician found that nothing he could say would persuade Aladdin to give him the lamp, he lost his temper. "Foolish boy!" he raged. "The treasure is yours but you will not live to enjoy it!" And muttering an incantation over the huge stone, he waited until it had dropped back over the entrance before striding away.

For two whole days, Aladdin was a prisoner in the well and, at last, convinced that he would starve to death, he pressed his hands together in an effort to remember one of his childhood prayers.

In an instant, a huge genie towered before him. "You have rubbed the ring, oh master, and now I am here to obey your commands," said the genie.

"Then take me to my mother," said the boy, too astonished even to feel afraid.

No sooner had he spoken than he found himself seated at the bare wooden table in his own kitchen and there, staring at him as if he had been a ghost, was his mother.

"Don't look so worried, mother!" Aladdin exclaimed. "Here I am safely back." Then he began to tell her the story of his adventure. "I don't believe that stranger was really my uncle," he concluded, "but a magician – though why he should want this dusty old lamp I can't think. Put it away in the cupboard, mother, for we don't have to think of selling it yet . . ."

"I'll give it a rub first," said his mother, when she had recovered from the strange story her son had told her.

Lo and behold, as she rubbed the lamp, there stood before them a gigantic creature – as tall as a house – but now bent almost double in deep obeisance.

"I am the genie of the lamp," said the spirit, in a deep, solemn voice, "and yours to command."

"Then bring us a meal fit for a Sultan," Aladdin ordered, as he put out an arm to support his terrified mother.

In a moment the bare wooden table was covered with silver and gold plates, piled high with delicious food.

The poor widow woman could scarcely eat a morsel – but not Aladdin! "No wonder he wanted the lamp!" he exclaimed, between mouthfuls. "Don't you understand, mother? The genie of the lamp will do anything he is asked to do. Now we can be as rich as the Sultan."

With the passing years, Aladdin did indeed grow rich and highly respected in the city. And, one day, he said to his mother, "I have seen the girl I mean to marry. She is the Sultan's daughter and as pretty as a flower."

"She can never be yours," said the old woman in a frightened voice. "Whoever heard of a poor tailor's son marrying a Princess?"

Aladdin laughed. "My genie will help me," he said confidently. "Go to the Sultan tomorrow and take with you some of the jewels I brought back from the cave. They will match any he keeps in his treasure store."

Now the Sultan valued precious stones above all else, and when he saw Aladdin's offering, he said, "My good woman, these jewels are indeed magnificent. Tell your son he may marry my daughter if he sends me forty large basins of pure gold filled with rubies and diamonds, each carried by a black slave. These are my terms."

The poor woman kissed the Sultan's feet and withdrew from his presence. Then she hurried home.

"The conditions are easily fulfilled," said Aladdin. And he took the lamp, rubbed it and so summoned the genie.

"It shall be done, master," said the genie, when Aladdin told him of his wishes.

The Sultan was so impressed, not only with the magnificence of the gifts, but by Aladdin himself, who headed the proces-

sion of slaves, that he readily gave his consent to the marriage.

Aladdin and his lovely Princess set up house in a palace as grand as that of the Sultan's and all went well until, one day, Aladdin went out on a hunting expedition.

He had only been gone an hour or two when a street trader began shouting his wares outside the palace. "New lamps for old! New lamps for old!"

"New lamps for old!" exclaimed the Princess. "I will please my husband with my thriftiness." And she ran out with the old dusty lamp, which she had found in one of the cupboards, and gave it to the trader, receiving in exchange a brand new lamp.

Alas, the trader, as you must have already guessed, was none other than the magician. No sooner was the lamp in his possession than he summoned the genie and ordered him to carry the palace and all its inmates to the African desert.

Aladdin was struck dumb with fear and dismay when he returned to find both his palace and his Princess missing. But he had little time to mourn his loss for, as he stood gazing at the empty space where his house should have been, soldiers arrived and dragged him off to face the irate Sultan.

"Miserable wretch!" thundered the

distraught father. "What have you done with my daughter?"

Now Aladdin had, by this time, guessed that the magician had got hold of the lamp. But, of course, he could not tell the Sultan what he thought had happened. Instead, he cried, "Give me forty days to find her!"

"If you fail," said the Sultan, "you will die."

As Aladdin wandered through the forest, he stumbled over a root and accidentally rubbed the ring he was wearing against the trunk of a fallen tree. In an instant, the genie of the ring appeared before him. "What is your command, master?" he asked.

"I know," Aladdin began, somewhat meekly, "that you are not as powerful as your big brother of the lamp. But take me to my Princess, wherever she may be!"

No sooner said than done! In a trice, Aladdin found himself in the presence of his young wife, as she stood before her mirror.

Quickly Aladdin told her about the lamp and the girl began to weep, blaming herself for the misfortune that had befallen them.

"All is not lost," Aladdin whispered. "I will procure a powerful sleeping powder which you must drop into his wine tonight. As he sleeps I will take the lamp from him."

That night, as Aladdin hid in one of the palace rooms, the Princess served the magician with the drugged wine, and no sooner had he drunk it than he fell to the ground.

Aladdin left his hiding-place and, upon searching the sleeping magician, found the precious lamp hidden about his clothing. In no time at all, he had summoned the

powerful genie. "Take us back to China," he ordered, "Let everything be as it was!"

Great was the Sultan's joy when, on looking out of his window, he saw once again his daughter's palace. And readily did he forgive Aladdin. So all ended happily for the young couple.

As for the wonderful lamp – that was hidden away in a place so secret that, after a few years, not even Aladdin himself could remember where he had put it!

The Real Princess

O NCE, LONG AGO, there was an old King who wished his son to marry.

"She must be a real Princess," he told the Prince. "You must search the world for her."

The Prince set out on his travels. He visited kingdom after kingdom, and he met a great number of beautiful girls. Many of them lived in palaces and spoke

and acted like real Princesses, but the poor young man could never make up his mind about any of them.

"Was she – or wasn't she?" he kept asking himself, until he began to doubt if he would know a real Princess when he saw one.

After a year of wandering from country to country, he became so unsure of himself that he returned home without a bride.

The King was bitterly disappointed that his son had failed so miserably in his quest, and the Queen said sadly, "We are both growing old. Our dearest wish was to see you happily married to a real Princess."

One night there came a dreadful storm of screaming wind and driving rain. As it raged about the castle, a gentle knocking was suddenly heard and the old King himself went to answer the door.

There, on the threshold, stood a tall young girl, drenched to the skin. Her fair hair was plastered to her face, hanging in wet strands about her shoulders.

No sooner had the surprised King invited her to step inside than she declared she was a Princess who had lost her way in the storm.

The Queen came to inspect their uninvited guest and was as surprised as her husband when, for the second time, the girl said she was a Princess.

"More like a waif," thought the Queen, looking at the rain-soaked girl. "But I have my own way of finding out the truth of what she says."

Without further questioning, the Queen

told the servants to prepare a room for their visitor. Then she hurried away to the kitchen, where she took a single dried pea out of the sack that lay there in the corner.

Before the chamber-maid had time to make up the bed, the Queen placed the pea on the bedstead and told her to fetch twenty mattresses. These were then laid on top of the pea.

Scarcely able to wait until morning the Queen was up before any of the servants. And when the young girl left her bedchamber, she was there to greet her.

"Did you sleep well?" she enquired.

"I did not," replied the girl. "There was a small hard object under the mattresses which bruised my skin and made sleep quite impossible."

On hearing this, the Queen broke into a happy smile. At last, she had found a suitable bride for her son! Only a girl of royal birth, a real Princess, could have detected something as small as a pea under twenty mattresses.

"Ah!" she cried, "I will take you to my son. You must meet him."

Well, it goes without saying that the handsome Prince and the lovely Princess liked each other almost immediately and before the end of the day had decided to marry.

After the wedding, the famous pea was not banished to the sack with the other, common peas, but placed in a small lacquer box and sent to the museum. On it, in letters of gold, were just two words: *Princess Detector.*

The Golden Goose

ONCE UPON A TIME there was a gentle, good-natured youth who was called Simpleton by his two smart brothers.

Now, sad to say, Simpleton's father and mother treated him just as badly as his brothers and his mother, especially, was forever wailing, "To think our youngest should have turned out to be such a big blockhead!"

Simpleton's father was a woodcutter and one day he asked his eldest son to go into the forest and cut down a certain tree.

"You can take some of my plum cake," said the fond mother, "and a bottle of good red wine."

The eldest son, whose name was John, shouldered his axe and set out, but the sun was hot and the forest very pleasant so, instead of starting to fell the tree at once, he sat down and took out the plum cake and the wine. As he ate and drank, a little wizened old man appeared before him dressed in green.

"I am hungry," said he, "and thirsty. Pray let me share your meal."

"Why should I?" demanded John. "I've scarcely enough here for myself." And he turned his back on the little man and went on with his meal.

But presently, as he began to hew down the tree, the heavy axe slipped and he cut his arm so badly that he had to return home.

"I'll go," said the second son. "You can trust me, father, to do a good job."

His loving mother gave him the best she had, which happened to be freshly baked apple-pie and a bottle of wine. And off he went.

When he reached the forest, he made up his mind, like his brother, to eat before starting to hew down the tree.

As he took out his apple-pie, the little scraggy old man appeared. "I am hungry," he said, "and thirsty. Pray share your meal with me."

"Ho! That's something I'm not willing to do," exclaimed the young man. "Go chase the squirrels!"

But, presently, as he started hewing down the tree, the axe slipped and he cut his leg so badly that he had to return home.

"I'll go! Please let me go!" Simpleton begged, when his father began wondering what to do.

"Never!" exclaimed his mother. "You'll chop your own head off, for sure."

But when Simpleton went on pleading to be allowed to try, his father said, "Oh, very well, off you go!"

And his mother gave him a stale bun, so hard that it would have bounced if Simpleton had dropped it, and a bottle of beer that had gone sour.

Like his two brothers before him, Simpleton decided to eat first and as he took a bite of the bun, along came the little green man. "I am hungry," said he, "and thirsty. Pray share your meal with me."

"Right gladly I will," said Simpleton, "though I'm afraid the bun is stale and the beer sour. But you're welcome."

The little man smiled and accepted the food and drink. To Simpleton's great astonishment, the bun suddenly tasted like his mother's richest plum cake and as for the sour beer, it was better than champagne.

"You have a kind heart," said the little green man, when the meal was over. "I'd like to do you a good turn. Cut down that old tree behind you and see what you find!"

Then he went off.

"I wonder what I shall find?" Simpleton asked himself, as he picked up his axe. And he went over to the tree and struck it a blow.

"Goodness me! What a surprise for Simpleton! There, inside, sat a fat goose – a fat *golden* goose!

"My, what a gorgeous creature you are!" he exclaimed in amazement. "Just one of your golden feathers would make

my fortune."

And he picked up the goose and tucked it under his arm. Then he set out for the nearest big town, thinking that he would find out the worth of his wonderful bird. But the town was quite a distance and so Simpleton decided to stay the night at the inn, which presently came into view, before continuing his journey.

As he entered, carrying his golden goose, the innkeepers' three daughters, plied him with food and drink.

"Help yourself to our finest cheese," said Kate, the eldest.

"Drink as much as you like," said Beth, the middle girl.

"You can have the best room," said Meg, the youngest.

But all the time they were talking to him, they were staring and staring at the golden goose.

"If only I had just one of these golden feathers," Kate was thinking to herself, as she cut the cheese, "I could sell it and with the money buy that new dress I've been wanting for so long."

And, of course, very similar thoughts were passing through the heads of her two sisters. But not by a look or a word did they give an inkling of what was in their minds.

Kate was the first to creep into Simpleton's room in the early hours of the morning. "Just one small feather," she told herself, as she reached out to grasp the bird's tail. But, oh dear me, when she tried to draw away her hand she found it was stuck fast to the goose.

As she began tugging and pulling, Beth tiptoed into the room.

"Don't – don't touch . . ." Kate whispered urgently. "The goose is . . ." But her warning went unheeded. Angry that her sister had got her hands on the bird first, Beth grabbed her shoulder, and she too found herself unable to pull away.

Then in came Meg. Both sisters tried to warn her. But Meg thought they were trying to trick her out of the golden feathers and she began pulling Beth away so that she too could get at the wonderful bird. Well, you can guess what happened! She stuck fast to Beth. So there they were – all three sisters unable to free themselves no matter how they tried.

Meanwhile, Simpleton slept on and when he did wake, he paid no attention to the three miserable girls. Tucking his goose under his arm, he ran downstairs and out into the road, and after him tumbled Kate, Beth and Meg.

As he strode along, the girls began wailing piteously for help. Now, it so happened that the old parson was early abroad that morning on his way to take a church service. When he saw the three sisters trailing after the young man, he took it into his head that they were pursuing him.

"Miserable, shameless hussies!" he said sternly. "Get back to your father's house!" And he grabbed the nearest of the girls, who happened to be Meg. Then he, too, was stuck fast.

As they passed the church, out came the curate, all in a flurry because the parson was late. "Hi! Your Reverence," he cried, running up and taking hold of his arm. "Have you forgotten the service?" And, lo and behold, he too was stuck fast.

Presently, as the strange procession neared the town, it was seen by two hefty road-menders.

"Come to our aid, good men!" cried the curate, and one of them put a big strong hand on his shoulder – and was forced to leave it there. His mate tried to pull his friend away and he too was stuck.

Not a single backward glance did Simpleton give as he walked steadily on. But as he entered the big town, he began whistling merrily as if to drown the shrieks, moans, wails and curses of the seven luckless people that followed behind him.

Now the King of the realm had his palace in this town. He also had a most beautiful daughter who, for two whole years, had been unable to smile. The King had spent a fortune on jugglers, clowns and jesters in a vain effort to bring even the teeniest smile to his daughter's solemn face, but without any success. At last, he let it be known that the first man to make his lovely daughter smile would win her hand in marriage.

There was a Notice to this effect on the town gates and when Simpleton saw it, he changed his mind about going to market. Instead, he made his way to the palace. Upon entering the courtyard, who should be sitting at the open window but the Princess herself!

My, what a sad, solemn face she had as she stared down! It had been fixed in a frown so long that it was little wonder the clowns and jesters had failed to make her smile.

But then, all at once, as she saw Simpleton trot round the courtyard with his seven followers all tumbling after him, the smallest, teeniest smile curved her lips. Then Simpleton began hopping and skipping and so too did the others for if they hadn't they would have tripped each other up. When he stopped suddenly so did they!

The Princess's smile broadened. Then she began to laugh. Oh, how she laughed!

On and on, until the King came rushing into her, thinking she might be in the middle of a fit.

Strange to tell, no sooner did Simpleton make the Princess laugh than the procession broke up and the sisters, the parson, the curate and the road-menders found themselves free to go their own way – which they did as fast as their legs would take them!

Then Simpleton went to the King. "I have made the Princess smile and laugh," said he. "So I have the right to marry her."

Now the King had no wish to see his daughter married to such an ordinary fellow as Simpleton, so he said, "Ahem, not so fast, young man. You must fulfil one or two conditions before you can marry my daughter. First, you must find me a man who will drink a hundred barrels of wine before morning."

Simpleton left the palace. Where could he look for such a man? A hundred barrels – why that was drink enough for a hundred men! Then he thought of his little old friend of the forest. Perhaps he would help him. So off he went. To his dismay there was no little man beside the ancient tree but there was a very large fat man, as round as a barrel himself, but with a sad face.

"Fat men," said Simpleton as he went up to him, "should look happy. But you look quite miserable. What's the matter?"

"I'm so thirsty," said the man, "I could drink the sea dry."

"Then come with me!" cried Simpleton. And he took him to the King's cellar and showed him the barrels of wine.

In the morning, when the King went to

his cellars, he found the barrels empty.

"Well," he said, hiding his anger as best he could. "Now, for my second task. You must find a man who will eat a mountain of bread before nightfall."

Once again, Simpleton thought of his old friend, and off he went back to the tree. There, he found a man as tall and thin as a pikestaff, and with a face as miserable as a rainy Saturday afternoon.

"What's the matter?" he asked.

"I'm starving hungry," replied the man. "I could eat a house."

"Come with me!" cried Simpleton, "and you can eat a bread mountain – that's better still!"

The King was more than a little angry when he found all the bread eaten. "Now," said he, "for the third task. If you succeed in building a ship that will sail on land as well as on water, my daughter is yours. I give you my promise."

To Simpleton's delight, the little green man was waiting for him when he reached the ancient tree. "Now," said he, "I need a ship that sails both on land and water."

"Your kind heart brings its own reward," said the little man. "Go back to the palace and I'll bring you such a ship."

When the King saw the marvellous ship he simply had to keep his promise and, before the week was out, Simpleton and the beautiful Princess were married. And a very happy and successful marriage it turned out to be!

Little Ida's Flowers

THERE WAS ONCE a little girl called Ida who didn't know very much about flowers. But then she had a birthday, and her mother gave her some flowers in a pretty pink vase and her grandmother gave her a pot of blue hyacinths and a pot of yellow tulips. Of course, Ida had all kinds of new toys as well, but it was the flowers that she noticed first as she ran in and out of the playroom.

At the end of her birthday week, Ida went into the playroom to give her flowers in the pink vase a drink – and they were all dead!

"My flowers that Mummy gave me are all dead," she thought, as she stared at them. "I must find someone to tell." But her mother was busy and her grandmother was shopping so she went out into the garden to look for Mr. Hobbs.

Mr. Hobbs was everybody's gardener. He was old and bent. He wore a battered straw hat on his head, summer and winter, and he had kind twinkly eyes.

Little Ida found him at the bottom of the garden, leaning on his spade.

"My flowers are all dead, Mr. Hobbs," she burst out. "I feel sad."

"I think you're flowers are just tired," said Mr. Hobbs. "I expect they would say, if you could understand their talk, that they had been dancing all this week up at the castle."

"What castle?" little Ida asked. "I don't know any castles."

"Ah, yes, well, you can't know everything," said Mr. Hobbs mysteriously. "But a lot of dancing goes on in the castle, I assure you."

"Do you really and truly think my poor flowers in their pink vase are just tired?" she persisted, beginning to smile.

"I do, I do!" said old Mr. Hobbs.

So then little Ida ran back to the house and upstairs into the playroom. "My flowers are not dead, just tired," she told her round-faced Dutch Doll, as she lifted her out of her cosy wooden bed, lined with blankets. "You won't mind, Sophy, if I put them in your bed. You'll have to sleep in the drawer."

She thought Sophy's face wore a scowl as she put her in the drawer and then laid the flowers carefully in the wooden bed, but it couldn't be helped.

When her own bed-time came round, little Ida looked at the blue hyacinths and the yellow tulips in their pots. "I expect you'll miss your friends tonight when you go dancing at the castle," she said. "But don't worry, I'm taking good care of them."

Then she went into the next room, into her own bedroom, and jumped into bed. But that night, Ida couldn't sleep for thinking about her flowers. She thought and thought until at long last she fell

asleep. When she awoke, a silvery moon had slid into the sky and was shedding its light into her room.

"I wonder if my flowers are sleeping?" she wondered, and then she thought she heard music, soft yet merry music, coming from next door.

"Who can be playing the piano?" she wondered, very surprised. And she got out of bed and crept to the door.

What a wonderful sight met her eyes! The hyacinths and tulips had left their pots and were standing in two rows in the middle of the room. And, dancing very gracefully in and out, were all kinds of other flowers whose names Ida didn't know.

At the piano sat a tall yellow lily which little Ida was sure she had seen growing in the garden in the summer. As she bent over the piano, her long yellow face reminded her quite strangely of her own music teacher.

None of the dancing flowers took the least bit of notice of little Ida and, presently, a large purple crocus went over to Sophy's wooden bed and spoke to the flowers lying there.

"He must have invited them to dance," thought Ida, as her flowers suddenly rose up and followed the crocus on to the floor.

Then she saw that Sophy was sitting up in her drawer. All the flowers, who had been resting in her bed, came over and began thanking her politely for her kind hospitality.

And Sophy said, "It was a pleasure." And she let herself down on to the floor for she wanted to dance.

"We shall all be dead tomorrow," the flowers told her. "But you must tell little Ida to bury us in the garden. If she does, we shall wake up again in the summer and be even more beautiful."

Then they kissed Sophy on her pink and white cheeks and invited her to dance with them.

Suddenly, as Ida watched from her corner, in came a great number of flowers

all very beautiful, but the most splendid of all were two wonderful roses wearing tiny gold crowns.

"They must be the king and queen from the castle," Ida thought. And all these poppies and peonies and carnations will be the lords and ladies of the court."

The tall yellow lily stood up and bowed and the dancers bowed and then the dancing continued.

"How very nice," little Ida told herself, "they've chosen to hold their ball here instead of in the castle."

At last the flowers wished one another goodnight and little Ida crept back to bed.

First thing in the morning she ran into the next room. There were the hyacinths and tulips back in their pots and her tired flowers still in Sophy's bed. Sophy herself looked very sleepy as she stared up at Ida from her drawer.

"You know you have something to tell me," said Ida. "You know what my flowers said. I have to bury them in the garden today so that they will look more beautiful in the summer."

And she fetched a pretty painted cardboard box out of the cupboard and put her flowers into it. Then she ran down to the garden, where she dug a little grave.

When the boy next door asked her what she was doing, little Ida told him all about her tired flowers, and he said, "They should have a proper burial service. I haven't a gun or cannon to fire in salute but I can shoot my arrows over their grave."

"That would be very nice," said little Ida. "I should like them to have something to talk about when I see them again in the summer!"

The Red Shoes

ONCE, LONG AGO, there was a pretty dark-haired girl called Karen. Karen was poor; she was so poor that she wore a dress with a big patch in the skirt and heavy wooden clogs on her feet. When her mother died, she was worse off than ever for now there was no one to take care of her.

"Poor little thing," said the cobbler's wife to her husband. "I'll make her a pair of red shoes out of some of our cloth."

The day Karen came to the cobbler's house to try on her new red shoes was the happiest in her life. Never had she seen such beautiful shoes, and to think they were hers!

But then other nice things soon began to happen to Karen. A rich old lady saw her in the village and offered to take her home.

Now she had new dresses to wear and plenty to eat and when the old lady took her into the town, she rode in a carriage. One day, as they drove past the palace, there was the young Princess walking with

the Queen.

How Karen stared! "She's not wearing her gold crown today," she whispered to her guardian. "She's wearing her red shoes, and look! They're just like mine."

And that night as she lay in bed thinking about the golden-haired Princess, it wasn't her big blue bows or the white dress with its frills that she remembered – it was her fine red shoes!

When Karen was old enough to be confirmed, the old lady said that she must have a new silk dress and a pair of new black shoes so that she would look just like all the other children in church on Confirmation Sunday.

The silk dress was easily found, but the old lady had grown weary of shopping. "You must choose the black shoes yourself," she told Karen, as they entered the expensive shoemaker's shop.

Now Karen knew very well that her kind guardian was both short-sighted and colour-blind and so, instead of choosing black shoes, she left the shop with a pair of red shoes, shiny leather red shoes that looked exactly like the ones the little Princess had been wearing.

How Karen loved her new shoes; she peeped at them a dozen times a day before Confirmation Sunday came round. But not once did she say to her kind old lady, "My new shoes for Sunday are red not black!"

Well, you can just imagine how the heads turned and the tongues clucked disapprovingly as Karen walked down the aisle that Sunday morning.

But Karen was not thinking about being in church or even trying to say her prayers as she knelt beside her old lady. She was thinking only of her red shoes.

As they left the church, an old sea-dog, with a beard as red as Karen's shoes and leaning on a crutch, stood there in the porch, begging for alms.

Karen thrust out her little foot so that he might see and admire her shoes, and the old sailor bent down and tapped each shoe with his rough weather-beaten hand.

"Pretty dancing shoes," said he. "Fit tightly and dance, dance, dance!"

Soon after that special Sunday, the old lady became very ill and there was no one to take care of her but Karen. And Karen had set her heart on going to a great ball which was being held in the town.

What would she do? Stay at home and take care of her kind old lady or go to the ball? Out came the red shoes and then the party dress! She would go to the ball!

Her red shoes danced her all the way to the ball and, once there, they danced her round and round until the fiddlers stopped their fiddling and everyone went home. But not Karen – for the red shoes took charge of her. When she should have turned right, they turned left. Across the silent Square they carried her and through the town gates.

"Stop! Stop!" she screamed, dreadfully frightened, but the shoes were stuck fast to her feet and would not come off.

Straight into a dark wood they danced her and there, among the trees, she

thought she saw the old sailor-man, nodding and pointing with his crutch at her dancing feet.

Through thorn and brier, Karen was compelled to dance until, with the first light of morning, she came to the church. And there, oh there, stood a tall shining angel.

"Help me!" cried little Karen. But the angel turned away and she knew, all at

once, that her kind old lady had died because she had not been there to take care of her.

Was there anyone who could help her? Only the executioner who cut off bad people's heads! "I have been selfish and vain," she cried, as she danced up to his lonely hut. "Come out and cut off my feet for I cannot come in."

And the executioner came out and cut off her feet. Away went the red shoes, dancing, dancing all on their own until they vanished from sight.

The tall shining angel was still there when Karen hobbled back to the church. No need to tell him she was sorry for he knew already. And as he smiled and beckoned her into church, Karen was suddenly happy – happier than when she had loved only her red shoes.

The Brave Little Tailor

ONCE UPON A TIME there was a little tailor who longed to be twice the size he really was. From morning to night he sat by his window, stitching and stitching and wishing that he was as big as a giant.

One morning, as he rested a moment from his tailoring, he saw an old peasant woman pass beneath his window. In her basket were some pots of delicious looking strawberry jam.

"Hi, there!" called the little tailor.

"Sell me some of your jam."

The woman did this gladly and soon the little tailor was spreading the rich, sweet-smelling jam on a very thick slice of bread.

But, oh dear me, the little tailor was not left in peace to enjoy his meal. Attracted by the jam, some pesty flies came in through the window. Buzz, buzz, buzz! Round and round they flew in their efforts to settle on the lovely strawberry jam.

"Shoo! Be off with you!" the little man shouted angrily. But the flies continued to bother him. Then, losing all patience, he took up a piece of cloth and with a lucky

swipe managed to kill seven of the flies with a single blow.

The little tailor looked down at the seven dead flies with pride. "Seven at one blow!" he exclaimed. "The world must hear of this." And he quickly cut himself a belt on which he embroidered the words, SEVEN AT ONE BLOW, in bright red wool.

Then without giving another thought to the mayor's new waistcoat he was stitching, he went over to his cupboard to see

what food he could take with him before going out into the wide world to seek his fortune.

Alas, the cupboard was almost empty except for a piece of old cheese and he took that and put it in his pocket. Then, with a proud smile, he fastened the belt round his thin waist, skipped over to the door and went into the street.

When his workshop was far behind him, the little tailor began following a road which led him through the countryside. As he went along he saw a small brown bird caught by its wings in a bush and, thinking he would do it a service, he gently set it free.

"I'll give you a ride," he told the bird. "You'll be safe enough in my pocket until you're strong enough to fly."

The road took him through a wood and over a hill and then seemed to go straight up into a tall mountain. Nothing daunted, the little tailor began climbing the mountain and when he reached the top, there – on a big boulder – sat an enormous giant.

If the giant hadn't been in a sitting position, he might never have noticed the little man. As it was, he roared, "You down there! What do you want?"

The little tailor looked up at the giant with no sign of fear. "Good day, friend," he began, "I'm just on my way to try my luck in the world. Would you care to be my companion?"

At this the giant gave a great laugh. Then he roared, "You – you grasshopper! How dare you speak to me in such a way?"

"I'll show you why I dare," replied the tailor, and he unbuttoned his coat so that the giant could read the words on his belt.

"Seven at one blow!" exclaimed the giant. And he looked at the little man with astonishment, thinking that the words

meant he had killed seven MEN with one blow.

"That's right," said the little tailor. "Seven at one blow!"

"I'd like to see for myself which of us is the stronger," said the giant at last. And he picked up a stone and squeezed it in his great hand until water dropped out of it.

"Simple!" exclaimed the tailor. "Watch!" And he brought out the lump of old cheese, which had grown soft in his pocket, and squeezed it until liquid oozed out of it.

At this, the giant, who was rather a stupid fellow, scratched his head and grunted, being at a loss for words. Presently, however, he picked up another stone and flung it with all his strength into the air. It went so high that the little tailor counted fifty before at last it dropped to the ground.

"Oh, well thrown!" said he. "But after all your stone did come down again. I'll throw one which you won't ever see again!"

And he took the little brown bird out of his pocket and threw it into the air. Rejoicing in its freedom, the bird soared high into the blue sky and vanished from sight.

"You're an odd little man and no mistake," said the giant. "But let's have one more test. Let's see who can lift the oak tree that's lying on the ground over there."

"Certainly," said the little tailor. "You take the trunk on your shoulders and I'll take the branches. I should think I'll have

After a few minutes, the giant gasped, "I'm going to lower the trunk!"

"And I'm going to lower the branches," replied the tailor, quickly jumping on to the grass before the giant had a chance to turn round.

Huffing and puffing, the giant stared when he saw the little tailor standing beside the head of the tree, smiling merrily and not a bit out of breath.

"You've proved your strength," the giant admitted. "I'd like to take you to meet my two brothers."

"Delighted, I'm sure," said the little tailor. "Nothing I'd like better."

The cave where the three giants lived was so big that the tailor thought it a palace compared to his small crowded workshop, and he smiled in a friendly fashion at the two giants seated by the fire, each with a roasted sheep in his hand.

"What is it?" asked the youngest of the giants, staring down at the tailor.

"A – a friend," his brother told him. "Give him something to eat and let him sleep in your bed for the night."

So the tailor was given a chunk of roasted sheep almost as big as himself and after he had taken a morsel, the youngest giant showed him the bed where he could sleep.

But as soon as their brother had told them how he had lost every trial of strength, the youngest cried, "We can't risk that grasshopper boasting to the world about this. We must finish him off tonight, but we'll wait until he's asleep."

Just as the fire was getting low, the youngest giant went over to the bed and gave it a mighty blow with his club. Then the three brothers went off to bed.

Imagine their astonishment, when early the next morning, they found the little man already up and seated at the table.

the heaviest load."

The giant groaned as he hoisted the trunk on to his broad shoulders and when the tailor saw that he could no longer look behind him, he hopped into the branches. So the giant staggered a few steps, bearing the whole weight of the tree and the little man as well!

"I trust you slept well," said he. "I slept very well indeed."

The little tailor had slept well but not in that colossal bed. Oh no! He had slipped out as the giants sat whispering by the fire, and lain down on a bear's skin in the darkest corner of the cave.

The giant's astonishment changed to fear when they saw the little man was not only alive but in the best of spirits! Away they thundered out of the cave and down the mountain, their hair standing on end.

"What odd fellows!" the little tailor thought, as he helped himself to some stew. "I wonder what was wrong?"

After breakfast, the tailor set out on his travels. Presently, he came to the court-yard of a royal palace and the grass was so inviting that he unbuttoned his coat and lay down. Soon he was fast asleep. As he slept, the Prime Minister chanced to come along and read the words on his belt. "Seven at one blow!" he read aloud. Then he thought how pleased the King would be to have such a warrior in his army.

"Just the very man we need," said the King, when the Prime Minister told him about the stranger. "See to it that he joins up right away."

So the little tailor was given a high rank in the King's army and of course this made all the generals and colonels very jealous.

"We won't serve under that little man," they told the King, after the first week. "He's not a proper soldier."

Now the King was afraid to tell the tailor to go. But he couldn't have an army without his generals and colonels. So at last he hit on an idea. Sending for the little tailor, he said, "Our kingdom is plagued by two terrible man-eating ogres known as Red-head and Black-Beard. I want you to kill them."

"I'll do that willingly," said the little tailor. "But what will be my reward?"

"My daughter's hand in marriage," said the King, thinking that the little man would certainly be killed by the ogres.

"Agreed!" cried the tailor, for the Princess was very pretty. "I'll set off now."

When he reached the dark forest where the ogres lived, he soon spied them fast asleep under a tall tree.

"My," thought he, "they're even bigger and fiercer than my first giants." But his courage did not fail him. As quiet as a mouse, he climbed the tree under which the ogres slept and slid along the branches until he was right above them. Then he took some stones out of his pocket and, Plonk! The first stone hit Red-head on the nose.

Red-head opened his eyes, rubbed his nose and glared at his companion. "That wasn't funny," he growled. "Stop it!"

His friend muttered sleepily. "What's that? Oh, never mind!" and dozed off again.

Plonk! Down came more stones, this time on Black-beard. Now it was the huge black-bearded giant's turn to wake up. "You just missed my eye," he roared. "Stop your games!"

"Tit-for-tat!" shouted Red-beard. And before you could say tailor's needle, the two ogres were at each other's throats.

Safely hidden in his tree, the little tailor watched as they began fighting, first with fists and then with tree trunks which they used as clubs. They fought so long and desperately that, at last, they killed each other.

When he saw the ogres were dead, the

tailor sprang down from the tree and ran off to tell the King.

"That's the end of your man-eating ogres," he said. "Now give me your daughter's hand in marriage."

The King hid his surprise and anger as well as he could. But he had to keep his word. And the very next day the tailor and the Princess were married.

Never in all his days had the little tailor had such an enjoyable time. Alas, one night he began dreaming about his workshop and speaking aloud in his sleep. "Bring me the yard-measure," he muttered. "The waistcoat must be finished."

His lovely young wife heard every word and, in great distress, she got out of bed and rushed straight to the King.

"I believe he's nothing more than a common little tailor," she told her father, beginning to weep.

The King re-assured his daughter. "I'll post my servants outside the royal bed-chamber tomorrow night," he told her. "They will take down every word he utters in his sleep."

But the quick-witted tailor had guessed why his wife had left him so suddenly in the night, for he remembered his dream most vividly. So the next night he only pretended to be asleep and dreaming.

"Bring me the yard-measure," he shouted. "My waistcoat must be finished. Have I not already killed seven at one blow? Do you want to be number eight?"

On hearing this, the servants fled in terror, and the Princess stroked her husband's hair and whispered that he was indeed her hero.

So all ended happily for the tailor. In time he became King, and no one ever guessed that the only creatures he had ever killed were seven little flies which happened to like strawberry jam!